The

Dark

Trails

Part II
A New Beginning

By William Deek Harris

Antioch, TN 37013

ISBN: 978-0-578-70029-8

Published William "Deek" Harris, Antioch, TN 37013

Printed in the U.S.A.

William "Deek" Harris, May 2020

WWW.DEEKHARRISBOOKS.COM

Chapter 1
The Road To Freedom

We traveled for nights under the cover of darkness to reduce our chances of being seen by white men looking for trouble or an easy payoff. We were less than a day's worth of riding before we reached Mr. Langford's property that I was to buy. We only had two near run-ins with white folks up until that point. Luckily for us, we were able to hear them coming and put out our lanterns before we were spotted. The last encounter was when we cross the path of a white man on a horse. His horse was running top speed until the fellow spotted our small wagon train. He raced up too fast for us to hide. Mr. Langford, Bella and I were heading the wagon train with our stagecoach. He spotted the light from our lanterns and road up to us. He was dressed in a dirt filled Confederate Army uniform. From the looks of him, he couldn't have been much more than a teenager in a grown man's army. His left hand was heavily bandaged with a dirty and blood-stained white rag. He stopped us and pulled out his pistol. The look on his face showed fear and uncertainty. He rode up on the right of our stagecoach where Mr. Langford was sitting and said "What are you doing out here by yourself with all of these niggers? Did they take you captive sir?" Slowly I began to slide my hand towards my pistol and Bella placed her hand over mine to stop me. I glanced down to see that she already had her derringer cupped in her hand ready to fire. "Oh, heavens no young man, I'm headed to my new land on the other side of Virginia. This is the last of my property that needed to be moved from my old home." The explanation didn't seem to set too well with the young soldier. He continued to make his way down the wagon train to the first covered wagon with Moses and his family sitting upfront. He stopped there and stared at Moses for a moment then looked down towards the back of the wagon train. He turned and came back to the front where we were. He looked at Bella then me and turned his nose up. He turned to Mr. Langford and asked, "Aren't you concerned about having your niggers back there by themselves? What if they decide to take off on you? You wouldn't even know." Mr. Langford smiled and said "Of course not. I treat them fair. They have no reason to go anywhere." The soldier smirked and nodded his head in agreement.

"So why are these two niggers sitting up front with you instead of with the other niggers? And why are they not dressed like the others?" Before Mr. Langford could respond Bella asked the guy, "Why is that a concern sir?" The young soldier whipped his head around to stare Bella in her eyes. "You allow your niggers to speak to white men like that?" he asked Mr. Langford without breaking his concentration on Bella. He raised his pistol and aimed at Bella. A sudden loud noise from one of the covered wagons drew his attention away from Bella. "What was that?" he asked. It seemed as though the woods had gotten quieter than it had ever been until another loud rustling noise echoed from the wagon. Quickly he rushed back to the train and stopped at the wagon behind Moses' wagon. He rode to the back of the wagon where he could hear the muffled sounds of distress coming through the wagon cover. He jumped off of his horse to take a closer look inside of the wagon. The closer he got to the back of the wagon the louder the noise became. He stood to the side of the wagon and used the barrel of his gun to slowly pull back one side of the wagon cover. He peeked inside and saw three people sitting with sacks over their heads with their hands behind their backs. "What's going on in here?" he asked. Then he used his bad hand to pull back the other side of the cover to get a full view inside. He was not expecting what his young eyes were seeing. "What in the hell is going on in here?" he asked, when he saw Jordan on the floor of the wagon wrestling with Jacob. "Is that a white man underneath that sack?" he asked Jordan. It was taking all that Jordan had to hold down Jacob's much bigger body. "He's a new slave that hasn't learned his place yet sir. But he will soon. He's gon be just fine soon enough." Jordan managed to get out while still struggling on top of Jacob. The young soldier looked closely and said "Horse shit! I can see by the color of his ankles that that's a white man you lying nigger!" He raised his gun then aimed it at Jordan and said, "I don't know what in the hell is going on in here, but you get your black ass off of him NOW!" He began to climb into the back of the wagon until he heard the clicking sound of me cocking my pistol. I placed the nose of the barrel behind his left ear and told him, "You seem to be hard of hearing. Do I need to open up your ear hole so that you can hear a little better? He said, 'he's a slave'. Now, so are you." All he could say was "Huh?" I smacked him in the back of the head with the butt of my gun and he went to sleep like a newborn baby. His body fell to the ground right at my feet. I stepped over his unconscious body then reached inside of the wagon and put Jacob to sleep the same way.

By the time the young soldier came to, we were arriving at our new home. "Well here it is. It's not much but this is what was left to me and now it can be yours for only twenty dollars." Mr. Langford turned and said to me as our stagecoach came to a halt. "There are six bedrooms, a library stocked with more books than you could read in a lifetime and a kitchen with more space than the entire house that Bella left behind. Every room in the house is fully furnished. When my aunt passed away years ago, she not only left me the house but everything in it as well. I had no desire to even come here let alone spend the manpower removing all of those things. And for one dollar more, all of the things inside are yours as well." he continued. The offer was more than generous. With all of the money that we had just taken from Scarlett and Hannah's plantation, I had more than enough to pay him. I knew that Mr. Langford was rich and dying but even for a rich man that was in his last days, it seemed crazy to just up and sell a house and hundreds of acres of land for such a small amount of money. "I don't know what you call much if you say that this isn't much. This house is huge", Bella blurted out with a smile. I laughed and said "Yeah Mr. Langford, I'd have to agree. This is no small house. Even the slave quarters are bigger than the hut I left behind too." He turned to me and said "Listen, if we're going to be living under the same roof you can drop the Mr. Langford crap and just call me Ronald or Ron. No need to remind me just how old I am." All I could do was shake my head and say "Ron it is." We began to head towards the house when we all heard Moses' daughter Asha scream out "Look!" She was pointing at a distant herd of wild horses she spotted galloping across the field and disappeared into the woods. They were being led by a beautiful solid black stallion. His muscles flexed and rippled with every gallop while his mane majestically waved in the air. Ten to fifteen more horses followed his lead but none as close as one black and white pinto mare. She was stride for stride with him. They immediately made me think of Bella and I. The fact that I was dark skinned and she was both black and white mixed seemed to be the perfect match. We were leading our people to a free and happy life just as the horses were doing with their herd.

My expression must have given away my excitement seeing the horse because Ron looked out to where the horses disappeared and said "That black horse is part of a legacy bloodline. My uncle tried for years to rope his father. He was unsuccessful and failed miserably. His father was all black just as he is and was just as beautiful. He would often come out into the middle of the field and stare at the house as though he was challenging my uncle. He could out run any of my uncle's other horses and was far smarter than them all, including my uncle. He even hired men to come bring that horse in and they all failed as well. One morning my uncle woke up to find the horse trotting around in the corral my uncle had made just for breaking this one particular horse. He went up to the horse to see if it would accept him but just as he was getting close one of the workers tried to lasso the horse and missed. The horse rose up on his hind legs and came down on top of my uncle knocking him to the ground. He began to repeatedly stomp my uncle in the head and chest until one of the workers shot it dead. Weeks later my uncle stepped out onto the porch to find an all black but much younger horse, standing in the middle of the field just like the other horse. It was obvious to my uncle that the horse left a son behind. He started calling this horse 'Devil Boy' because he swore that the horse was the spirit of the first horse coming back to haunt him. He never tried to rope him though. I don't know if he was afraid of the horse or if he felt remorse for being the reason the young colt lost his pappy." I was fascinated by Ron's story but even more fascinated when Devil Boy trotted back out from the woods and stood in the open field alone. He stared at our small wagon train for a moment then was joined by his mare. She looked for a moment then turned to head back into the woods. He slowly followed her but stopped at the edge of the trees to rise up on his hind legs and kicking his front legs high in the air. I'm not sure if it was a warning to stay away or if it was a challenge. I took it as a challenge as I watched him run off into the woods to join the others.

Chapter 2
From A House of Hell To A Home

Half of the first day at our new home was mostly spent allowing everyone to choose a house out of the twenty-five abandoned slave quarters on the huge plantation. Many of the old homes were twice the size of the slave quarters they lived in before I gave them the opportunity to be free and work for me like humans instead of animals. But from the time we all set fire to Hannah and Scarlett's plantation, you could see the sense of freedom in their eyes. I also knew that it was up to me to provide them with a safe place to live as I promised. Luckily Ron's promise of selling me the hundreds of acres of land and home would help me to keep that promise. The other half of the day was spent having our new white slaves cleaning and mending repairs to the main house. It was apparent that they had never had to work so hard a day of their lives. They were accustomed to being on the other side of the whip instead of it being the other way around. Jacob was the most rebellious of course. He hated the fact that Moses was now his overseer. It didn't help Jacob any knowing that Moses was also using the whip that he once owned and used on Moses and the others. Jacob soon had more than he could handle from Moses and the whip that he once used to rule over the black slaves in the past. His initial acts of defiance fueled Moses' pleasure in unleashing his wrath on Jacob and watching the fear in the eyes of the other white slaves. It was a look of terror that Moses once had in his own eyes and the eyes of many others that were witnesses to Jacob's years of torturing. The reality of their new lives as slaves began to sink in quickly. Things were no longer in their favor now that the tables had been turned. Never in a million years would they have ever thought they would see the day that blacks would be free and owners of white slaves. More importantly, they never would have imagined that they would be slaves themselves. Regardless to how farfetched it seemed, this was now their reality whether they liked it or not. After watching my entire family murdered at the hands of evil slave catchers when I was just a teenager, I had absolutely no remorse for the life ahead of them.

That night we chained all of the white people up in one of the smallest houses with two of the former black slaves guarding them. It was a long day and many more ahead of all of us before the entire place would be fully restored. Bella and I shared a huge bedroom upstairs in the main house. It had the biggest bed that I had ever seen. The whole house was decorated with a bunch of fancy white folks stuff even fancier than Hannah and Scarlett's home. That night while everyone else was fast asleep I found myself sitting on the top step of the porch that wrapped around the entire house. I was just as tired from working as everyone else but my mind was still racing with ideas of what my next move would be when everything was all set. The possibilities were endless. I thought of so many things that I could do to keep the place running but my thoughts were interrupted by an unexpected visitor. Had it not been for the rolling clouds freeing the rays of light from the full moon, I probably never would have seen him. But none the less there he was, standing in the middle of the field watching me. It was the stallion from earlier. He was too far away to see directly into his eyes but I didn't need to because I could feel him looking at me. I stood up and started to walk off of the porch then heard "He's not going to just let you just walk up and start riding him you know?" It was my dear Bella. I was so captivated by the beauty of this horse that I didn't even hear Bella come out of the house. "Of course not. But I will ride him." I replied smiling without ever turning around. "A horse like that is too smart and proud to just let someone walk up and break him. I'm going to have to work for him, and hard too." I added. "It doesn't have to be hard" she said as she began to walk down the steps. I turned around and she stopped on the step just above me so that we were eye to eye. "What do you mean?" I asked. She looked at me with her beautiful brown eyes then wrapped her arms around my neck and said "Cody what would you do if someone took me away? Would you come for me or do nothing?" I placed my hands around her waist and answered "What do you think? Of course, I would come for you." She smiled and gave me a little peck on the lips. Then she asked "What if I couldn't go? Would you stay?" At first I was confused at her questions but then it hit me like hammer. "So, what you're saying is, if I get his female then I can make him come to me?" I questioned even though I knew that's what she meant. Her facial expression slowly went from a sneaky grin to a soul piercing stare. She said "But don't underestimate her. She may not put up as big of a fight as he will, but she is going to fight and like hell. But once we break her it will be worth the battle." I leaned back from her then chuckled and said, "What do you mean 'once WE break her?' I will get a couple of the men to help me. Besides, I don't want you to get hurt. Wild horses can be dangerous." She gave me a smirk and said "Were you concerned about me getting hurt when I stabbed that man in the saloon to save you and Moses? No! Were you concerned when we robbed the gun store together? NO! You weren't concerned at all when we went to take over and burn down the Starr plantation! So, don't start now." All I could do was hang my head and slowly shake it. But little did she know…I was concerned during everyone of those times. I knew what she was getting at so I accepted her point. She placed her finger under my chin and raised my head and smiled then said "You once told me that your mother was a strong woman that could do anything that any man could do. God didn't stop making strong black women after your mother. I'm one as well sweetie. Besides, I need a horse for me. And she's mine!" Then we kissed like it was our very first time kissing each other. When we finished and opened our eyes, we looked out into the field and both horses were standing there watching us. The male raised high up on his hind legs then his mate turned and galloped off through the trees. He stood there for a moment then took off to join her. Bella smiled and said, "See, they're inseparable … just like us!"

On the way inside of the house we were greeted by Ron. He was standing in the door with a half-filled glass of whiskey in his left hand and a half-filled bottle of the rest in his other hand. "What are you doing up?" I asked him. He took a sip from his glass then used his shirt sleeve to wipe his snow-white beard and mouth. It was clear that it wasn't his first drink. He staggered towards us and shoved the bottle into my chest. "I've been up thinking" his raspy voice slurred. The scent of whiskey on his breath was strong enough to get me drunk by itself. I took the bottle and put my arm around his shoulder to make sure that he didn't fall to the floor. I walked with him into the library and led him to have a seat in a chair. Bella found great humor in Ron's drunkenness. She laughed then gave me a kiss on the cheek and said, "I'm going to let you handle this one alone. I've had more than my fair share of nights like this with him. He's all yours. I'm going to sleep. Goodnight honey." I could hear her giggling and laughing on her way up the stairs. As soon as we heard Bella close the bedroom door Ron sat back in the chair then crossed his legs and downed the rest of his drink of whiskey. He sat his empty glass on a small round table that sat next to him. Ron reached across the table and patted the arm of another chair for me to have a seat with him. I took the seat as he requested. He stroked his beard and asked, "So Cody, now that you have all of this money that we took from Hannah, what are your plans?" I thought for a second and realized that I didn't have one. I never had any real money to have to make any real decisions. "I'm not sure." I answered then I took a drink of whiskey straight from the bottle. Ron grabbed his glass and extended it my way to pour him another drink. I poured the drink for him and took another from the bottle for myself. Ron sipped his drink then said, "You're not going to be able to put all of that money in a bank without drawing some suspicion. You're going to have to be smart about everything that you do in order to keep what you have." He shifted his body in his seat to face me and added, "You know the cold weather will be coming soon and now you have more mouths to feed. All of the people you freed and promised a better life are going to need help. They have been used to a white master telling them what to do and how to even live. You have a strong Indian background full of survival knowledge that can provide and educate everyone. There's plenty of land for crops and livestock to feed everyone. I can go into town and buy the necessary materials without being questioned the way you would. That's no problem. In a couple of days, I can take Jordan and a couple of the other men to town with me. We can get some of the seeds for crops and building materials. However, you're going to need more hands to do the work. Soon we're going to have to get more white workers to make this less work on you. I can also check on some of the slave owners that were there when I was a kid. There's one in particular that I would love to see end up on the other side for the rest of his life as well as his brother."

<u>Chapter 3</u>
<u>Whitestock</u>

That next morning there was a knock at our bedroom door. "Who is it?" Bella screamed at the door. "It's me Ms. Bella, Moses' daughter Asha." Bella got out of bed and went to the door. When Bella opened the door. Asha was standing there with a look of fear on her young face. "What's wrong darling? Is everything ok?" Bella asked. Asha began to shake her head frantically. "No, it's not. My mother said to come and get you right away. One of the men tried to escape last night. They have him tied to a tree right now. Please hurry!" Asha explained and then ran out of the room. Bella and I quickly got dressed then rushed outside to find the others. When we got outside, we found everyone standing around a tree shouting and cursing at the runaway. We made our way through the crowd to find the young white soldier with his arms wrapped around a huge tree with his hands tied together. He was yelling just as loud back at the crowd and even attempting to spit on people. Moses was standing behind the soldier with his whip ready to lay into his backside. The crowd was egging Moses on to whip him. I walked up to Moses and asked, "What's going on here big man?" Moses turned to me and said in his deep voice "Last night while everyone was asleep this one tried to escape. He used his Army knife to cut his rope. He must have had the knife hidden on him somewhere. Luckily, I had two men sitting outside their house keeping guard. He knocked one of them down and was able to get away for a bit. He ran into the woods, but they were able to get him back. If they are truly going to be slaves then we have to treat them the way they treated us when we were slaves." Without warning Moses reached back and unleashed three blood drawing lashes to the back of the soldier. The young soldier yelled out "Nigger!" after the third lash. Moses drew back to issue yet another blow from his whip when I stopped him. "Wait!" I said as I grabbed his hand before it could come forward again. "What is his name?" I asked Moses. He shrugged his shoulders but never lost the deeply embedded scowl on his face. I walked over to the young soldier and asked him "What is your name soldier?" He looked me up and down with a glare of pure hate then said "I ain't telling you shit nigger!" I smiled and looked away and asked, "Is that right?" Before he knew what was happening, I grabbed him by the back of his stringy dirty blonde hair and slammed his face into the tree. I turned back to him and said, "Now I'm going to ask you again. What is your name boy?" He turned to me in a daze and said "Fuck you! Tell me your name." then spat a mouth full of blood and his front tooth on my boots.

My first instinct was to pull out my gun and blow the back of his head across the yard but that would have been too quick. I wanted him and the other white racists to suffer the life that they had put my people through. Since I decided to spare his life, I felt that I should let him in on what his future now held. I walked around to the other side to face him and said, "You still don't get it do you?" A look of confusion consumed his face. "Who are you? And what makes you think you can get away with keeping good wholesome white folks like us tied up like slaves? You're going to hang for this nigger!" I laughed then slowly walked around him again until I was back to the other side of him again. I looked him in the eyes and said "Those are all good questions and I have a good answer for them all. First of all, my name is Cody Black but you and the rest of the white folks over there will call me…MASTER!" Then I slammed his face into the tree again. Hannah and her mother Scarlett were standing only feet away begging for me to spare his life. The four white men, Franklin, Overton, Jacob and his son Travis were all standing helplessly filled with anger at how we were treating him. I pointed over to them and told the soldier "Do you see those so called 'good wholesome white folks' as you called them? Well the two women over there owned and operated a slave plantation that held all of these beautiful black people against their will for years until I came along with my woman Ms. Bella Rose and her good friend Mr. Ronald Langford. We gave them their freedom and offered them an opportunity to come live in peace. And to answer your other question, we plan to get away with it because no one knows that we are here. No one knows that YOU are here. Look around, there's no one for miles and I now own all of the land as far as you can see. That means we can do whatever the hell we want to and with you as we please. You can scream as loud as you want but no one can save you now." His scowl soon turned to a look of concern when reality set in and he realized that what I was saying was true. He lowered his head and I could tell that all of his tough talk had run out. His lips began to quiver then he raised his eyes and asked "So what are you going to do to us? Are you going to kill us?" I chuckled and said "Oh no. I'm going to treat you the way white folks have been treating blacks for ages. You are now my slaves. You will learn what it feels like to have your life filled with pain and suffering just as they made these people feel. And you will know what kind of life you and your army are fighting so hard to keep people like us living! I also know that you deserted your army. So, I really don't give a damn what your name is because even your army knows it's not worth a shit by now. From now on your name is Coward!" He quickly held his head up and began to scowl again as if he had all of a sudden found his toughness again. "FUCK YOU

28

NIGGER!" He yelled at me. Again, I grabbed him by the back of the head and slammed his face into tree. The jagged edges of the tree bark ripped through the skin on his face like a serrated blade of a saw. I walked off leaving him half standing and barely able to speak. As I walked away, I could hear him mumble "My name is Daniel Starks. I am a Private and you can't do this to me." I stopped walking and never looked back at him then said "Not anymore! Your name is Coward like I said. And there's no one to stop me from getting away with this." I walked up to Moses and told him "Give him ten more licks then cut him loose. When you're done, put his ass straight to work with the rest of them." Then I headed back to the house with Bella on my arm and Ron following right behind us. As we walked away, I could hear the sound of the whip cracking followed by the blood gurgling screams coming from Coward.

That night after dinner I went to sit on the porch and took a seat in one of the four rocking chairs just to see if the horse would show up again. After sitting there for over an hour he never showed up but I still had company to join me. The front door opened and out stepped both Bella and Ron. Bella took a seat in the chair to my right and Ron took the one on my left. "So why are you sitting out here alone?" Ron asked. "He's waiting for the horse of his dreams to show up." Bella answered before I could say a word for myself. All I could do was smile at the fact that she knew me so well in such a short time. I turned to Bella and placed my hand on hers then said, "I waited for the woman of my dreams and now she sits right next to me. And soon the horse of my dreams will be mine as well." I raised her hand and gave it a gentle kiss. Her face began to glow as she looked deeply into my eyes. "Well that's cute and all but you need more than a horse. You need hands…working hands. After this morning's events I got to thinking more about those brothers I told you about last night. We may need to pay them a visit sooner than later. I'll take Jordan in town with me tomorrow to do a little shopping for supplies and snooping for information" were the words from Ron that snapped us out of our entrancing love stare. He stood to his feet then faced us and said "I'm going to bed now. I'm going to need some money for supplies. I will see you before we leave. Goodnight you two." Ron advised as he made his way back inside and left us alone on the porch. Bella looked at me with a huge smile and asked, "Earlier today you referred to me as 'your woman'. Did you really mean that?" I grabbed her hand and raised it to my lips then kissed it and said, "With ALL of my heart!" She began to blush then said "Well come upstairs and show me. Make me believe that I'm yours." Then she stood and walked over to the front door. She put her right foot just inside of the door and placed her left hand on the door framed then leaned against it, separating her fluffy breast. "Prove it to me Cody. Come prove to me that I'm yours," she requested in a low sexy voice. Then she walked inside leaving the door open for me to follow her. She knew that I could not resist her beautiful brown eyes and short curly hair. I didn't hesitate to follow her to give her just what she was asking for.

Early the next morning Bella and I were awakened again by a knock on our bedroom door. After a long night of making love, Bella was still fast asleep and never even budged when the knock came. I rolled out of bed and walked over to the door. "Who is it?" I asked trying not to awaken my sweet Bella. "It's me!" answered the voice on the other side. This time it was Ron. I opened the door and stepped out into the hallway with him. "Top of the morning to you, young man," he said rocking back on his heels with his thumbs wrapped around his suspenders. I'm not much of a cheerful morning type of person. I scratched my crotch, folded my arms and stared at him. I'm sure that if he didn't know already, then he learned from the look on my face. He cleared his throat and said

"I've asked Jordan to gather two other men to ride into town with us. We shall be gone for a couple of days. Moses and the others will stay behind to oversee your whitestock." Immediately I stopped him and asked, "My what?" With a smirk on his face he answered, "Your whitestock. So technically they are now white slaves, but this seems to fit them. They're of course white. But now they're your property like livestock. I just put the two theories together and came up with…whitestock." I thought for a second and told him "I like it. From now on here at 'The Black Rose Ranch', that's what we will refer to them as." Ron stroked his beard and looked up as though he was thinking and said "The Black Rose Ranch eh? I see what you did there. You took the last name of you and Bella and named your estate. I like that as well. It's clever." I smiled and responded "Thank you. You're not the only one that's been thinking of names. But you didn't get me out of bed with my woman just to swap names. I know that you really came for money to get the things that I need. Give me moment and I will bring it out to you." Ron nodded his head and I walked back into the bedroom. After Bella and I finished making love the night before, I went ahead and pulled it out of my hiding spot because I knew that he would be coming for it. I walked back out of the room and handed Ron a fistful of money. "Here you go. This should be more than enough to cover the cost of what you need. While you are in town, I'd like for you to get a safe as well, so I don't have to keep running outside every time I need money. Use what you have left to pay Jordan and the other men that are going with you. I'm sure they will appreciate receiving pay for working now." Ron smiled and said "As you wish. We shall return in two days Mr. Black." He turned and walked off waving the money in the air over his head shouting "You're a good man Cody Black, a GOOD man!"

<u>Chapter 4</u>
<u>The Trip Into Town</u>

The two days that Ron was gone felt more like two weeks, but they finally return with everything that I requested and more. Ron and Jordan rode up in the fancy stagecoach while the other two men trailed right behind them in a covered wagon. It was around the middle of the afternoon and I was in much need of a well-deserved break from making repairs around the ranch. I noticed that only one of the men was sitting up front on the wagon. I stepped down from the porch to greet them. "Welcome back home!" I yelled out to them with my arms stretched out. Jordan hopped down and assisted Ron with getting down as well. Grinning from ear to ear Jordan rushed over to me and placed his hands on his hips then said, "Mr. Cody you gon' be real pleased when you see what we got you…real pleased. Come see!" Ron walked over to the wagon and we followed. While we were walking up to the wagon the driver stayed in his seat and gave me a big smile then nodded his head. "How do Mr. Cody?" he said. I smiled and answered, "I'm doing fine my friend and you?" His eyes grew big and he said "I feel alive for the first time in my life. Thanks to you Mr. Cody." His sweaty smiling face glowed with freedom and purpose. We got to the back of the wagon and I discovered that the other man was in the back with the same glowing smile, holding a pistol. He was pointing it at a white man with a sack over his head and hands tied behind his back. Not only did they get the supplies that we needed but they also managed to come back with new whitestock. I reached inside of the wagon and slowly removed the sack. The white man was afraid and trembling like a leaf in the wind. Tears began to cover his face and a smirk covered mine. He had the same look of terror that I had seen many times on the many faces of black slaves. "What do we have here?" I asked aloud. Jordan was quick to answer, "This one here we spect is a slave catcher. We found him in the woods on our way back home. We stopped a ways back where he couldn't see us but we could see him through the trees. Probably never would have even known he was there if it hadn't been for his grunting and cussing. He was swinging a big tree branch over his head and coming down with it like he was chopping wood. At first I couldn't see what he was hitting on the count of him having his back to us. So, I gets off the stagecoach and slowly walks up to him real quiet like. When I got closer, I saw the most awfulest thing in the world Mr. Cody." Jordan's head dropped and began to get choked up. I looked at Ron and he took his hat off then held it with both hands close to his chest. Ron's head lowered and he said, "He was standing over the body of young girl that he must been chasing. He was bashing her head in with a large tree branch. She was already dead by the time we found them. He was so worried about killing the po girl that he didn't even hear Jordan walk up on him." That's when Jordan's eyes looked up at me and he said, "I was going to shoot him, but Mr. Langford yelled out, 'don't kill him.' He deserves to die for what he did to that child Mr. Cody! She was just a BABY!" Without any warning Jordan lunged with both arms reaching to get his hands on the guy. Ron dropped his hat to the ground and grabbed Jordan before he could make it inside of the wagon. The guy jumped forward with his faces sticking out of the back of the wagon and yelled "Keep him away from me. He's crazy!" I looked back over my shoulder at him and back handed him in the mouth before either of us even realized what happened. The guy fell backwards on his ass. I leaned in and said "He's not the one that you need to worry about. He's not crazy. He's angry. But me, I'm crazy!" I grabbed him by his hair and dragged him out of the wagon and straight to the ground with him screaming like a little girl. I had the men to put him to work immediately with the rest of the whitestock before I killed him myself.

After dinner Bella and I decided to relax in the library and share a cigarette and drink of whiskey. I took a seat behind a large desk perfectly placed across the room facing the door. Bella sat in the chair across from the desk. It didn't take long for Ron to find us. He walked in holding a piece of paper in his left hand while his right hand held on to his suspender by his thumb. Ron sat the piece of paper down on the desk and stabbed it with his index finger then said, "THAT'S who we need to bring in to add to the whitestock." Bella grabbed the paper from under his finger and asked, "What are you going on about now old man?" Ron held up his fist and squinted his eyes then growled "That's one of the men I was telling you that we need to see. Harry Matthews and his brother Terry are two of the biggest slave traders in the area. No one brings in slaves without them having their hands in it somewhere. Their family and my family were good friends when I was younger. Their family has made a fortune off of the backs of slaves for generations. Someone needs to put an end to their business." I sat up in my seat and asked, "What is that and where did you get it?" Ron responded "It's a bounty poster taken off of the fella we brought in today. Moses and the others couldn't read it, but they knew what it meant when they saw the sketch of the girl on it. Which reminds me, we need to teach them how to read and write as soon as possible." Bella tossed the paper back onto the desk and said, "Men like them are not going to be as easy to get to as it was Hannah and Scarlett. They probably have way more men than we can fight. We'll have to be extra careful. We'll need a plan and a good one to pull something like this off. Hell, we need an army." I stood with pride and a smile on my face then said, "We have one." Bella frowned and asked, "And where is this army?" I stepped from behind the desk and took a seat on the corner of the desk then said "They're right outside my dear Bella. I taught Moses how to shoot, didn't I?"

That's when Ron chimed in with his finger raised "WE taught Moses how to shoot. And he's right. We can do it and I know just how to pull it off. However, I'm going to have to go back into town to turn over some old stones for a bit of information. If I'm correct, then we will have at least a couple of months to prepare. But either way we need to get started on teaching as many men as we have how to shoot. They'll need to learn sooner or later anyway." Ron headed out of the library then stopped at the door. He turned and said "As a matter of fact, I think I will go tomorrow. No need of waiting." I nodded my head and asked, "Do you want someone to go with you?" He shook his head then laughed and said, "No no…this is a trip that I need to make alone." Then he walked out. Bella laughed and said "That old fart is up to something. I can feel it!"

<u>Chapter 5</u>
<u>I See Myself In Him</u>

The next morning Ron hit the trail early to head back into town. Bella and I got up early enough to see him off. We stood and watched Ron ride off with one of the covered wagons instead of his fancy stagecoach. We could only imagine what he was up to. When we turned around, we saw Moses and Jordan walking up to us. "Where's he headed?" Jordan asked. "Well good morning to you too." Bella responded showing her disapproval of Jordan's rudeness. Jordan quickly snatched his hat from his head and clenched it tightly with both hands then said with a huge grin, "Pardon me Ms. Bella. Morning to you and Mr. Cody." Bella smiled with satisfaction as a mother would that was keeping her child in order. "Now that's better. I'm headed back inside. I'll leave you men folk to tend to your manly business." She gave me a kiss on the cheek then walked off. I watched Bella walking away with a smile on my face. Her hips had a way of putting me in a trance when I saw her from the back. I probably would have watched her all the way into the house if Moses hadn't broken my trance with, "So where did Ron go?" I turned my attention back to the two of them and answered "He's going back into town to get a little more information on the new guy's boss. He'll be back in a couple of days or so. Meanwhile, we need to put some of the tools and material that we have to work. We need to have crops planted as soon as possible. The food you guys brought back will only last for so long and I don't want to keep sending people in town too often yet. It's too dangerous." They both nodded their heads in agreement. I pointed out the areas that needed to be plowed for the crops and they headed off to get started. The fact that they were now going to have the chance to make white folks work hard in the field was a dream come true. They were more than ready to get started.

While Moses and Jordan were off making sure the field got taken care of, I took the opportunity to inspect the abandoned horse stable and corral behind the main house. The corral appeared to still be in good shape, which was no surprise, considering the fact that Ron's uncle didn't really get to use it much. After checking all of the posts and planks, I was convinced that it was ready for work. Next I walked over to check out the huge stable to see what it had to offer. It was almost as big as the main house. I walked up and pulled open one of the large double doors. There were ten individual stalls in a row on each side with enough space between them for two wagons to ride side by side and still have extra space. Overhead was a loft that stretched and wrapped around the entire stable used to store hay. The stable was fully stocked with saddles, horse blankets, brushes, ropes and anything else that you would need to take care of a horse. I began to walk down the long row and stopped about halfway inside when I heard some rustling noises in the hay. I pulled out my pistol and slowly began to walk towards the sound. The closer I got to the sound I heard heavy breathing mixed in as well. At the halfway point of the stable, the rows were separated after the fifth stall by an opened area for grooming and tending to the horses. Then the other five stalls start on the other side of the work area. It was in that work area to the right where I could hear the sound. I stepped around the corner and raised my pistol the cocked the hammer back. There was no way I was going to let some white man come onto my land and take it. When he heard the sound of me cocking my gun, he dropped the pitch fork he was holding, and threw both of his hands high in the air. "PLEASE DON'T SHOOT!" he cried out. Then he slowly turned to face me. I lowered my pistol when I realized it was one of the young men we freed from the plantation. "What are you doing in here boy? I almost blew your head clean off your body." I told him. I put my gun back in my holster and he lowered his hands. A look of relief was all over his face when he saw that it was me. We both thought that we had encountered an uninvited white man looking for trouble.

Once we both relaxed and realized that neither of us were a threat to the other, I pointed to a pair of stools sitting next to a work bench. He took a seat on one and I sat on the other. "What's your name?" I asked. He placed his hands on his hips then smiled and said, "My name is Charles, Masta Cody." His words brought me out of my seat. I hopped to my feet and barked at him "I AM NOT YOUR MASTER! You and your family are free to leave at anytime. Now tell me, what master would allow you and your family to go as you please?" A look of fear and uncertainty covered his face. He hung his head then said, "I don't have any family. It's just me in the world." All of a sudden, I didn't feel so offended, rather than shame. Shame for attacking him the way I did. It was clear to me then that he was far too conditioned to being a slave to know any better and too young to understand that I was no different than he. He slowly raised his head to look at me. "Where is your family?" I asked in a much calmer voice. Once more he lowered his head then answered, "They're all gone. The masta I was with before Ms. Scarlett was down right out evil. He raped my mother one day while my father and I were working in the field. My mother was a really pretty woman with light colored skin like Ms. Bella. So, she got to work inside the big house serving the family. I remember it like it was yesterday. My mother's friend, Ms. Ella, came running out to the field to get my daddy. I can still hear her voice in my head yelling, 'Amos come quick. Masta George forced himself on Mary Anne and she stabbed in the leg with a letter opener. You need to hurry before he kills her.' Daddy and me runs as fast as we could to the big house. Now masta George didn't allow no field niggers in his house but that wasn't stopping my daddy nor me. Daddy's legs were much faster than mine, so he got there a lot faster than me. Daddy rushed up the steps and before he could get to the front door there was the sound of a gunshot inside the house. It froze us all in our steps. Momma staggered out of the house trying her best to get away. The top of her dress was covered in her own blood. Masta had shot her in the stomach. She fell on the floor of the porch with her hand reaching out to my daddy. She slowly started crawling to daddy but masta George stepped out before she could even reach the top step. Daddy had started running for momma but stopped when masta came out holding his gun in his hand. He stood over my mother and looked out at my daddy then shot my mother in the back of her head. Daddy screamed 'Nooooo' and took off running for masta George. He let my daddy get about three or four steps from the top and blew my daddy backwards. Daddy was dead before he even hit the ground. I tried to run over to them, but Ms.

Ella wrestled me to the ground and stopped me. She held me down until two of my daddy's friends came and grabbed me. They knew that if I had gotten loose that masta would have shot me too. I knew it too, but I didn't care. The next day masta had me taken into town and put on the auction block. That's how I ended up with Ms. Scarlett and then you came."

Again, his words did something to me but this time they hit close to home instead. He and I had a lot in common. We both watched our families murdered right in front of our eyes and left in the world alone. I understood his pain, his hatred, the sense of being alone and everything that he was going through. I placed my hand on his shoulder and told him, "I'm really sorry to hear about your family. I lost my family years ago." A tear rolled down his face and quickly he wiped it attempting to be strong. I pulled him close to me and gave him a much-needed hug. That's when he let his tears pour into my chest. I allowed him to let it out because I could tell that he had been holding it in much like I once did. Once he was done, he stepped back and said "I didn't mean to upset you when I called you masta. I really didn't know what to call you." I smiled and said, "You can just call me Cody." He wiped his eyes and smiled then said "Ok…Cody." There was a look of relief on his face that looked much better than the look of terror he had at the beginning of our conversation. "So why are you in here instead of with the others?" I asked. He smiled and said "Well you see, I've always loved horses. Growing up I used to get to work with the horses until I got big enough to help out more in the field. But every chance I got, I would always spend as much time as possible with the man that took care of the horses. He was actually kind of nice. He taught me a lot about horses and what they needed. He showed me just about everything he knew. So when I got to Ms. Scarlett's, Moses saw how good I was with the horses that he convinced masta to let me work in the stable instead of the field on the count of me knowing so much and them not having anyone that knew as much as me. And when we got here Moses says I can take on this stable and get it right the way I saw fit. So that's what I was doing. Right now I needs to get rid of all this bad hay. It's not fit for them to eat. This here will have a horse sicker than a man drinking old milk." I took a look around and noticed that there was a lot of hay that needed to be removed. It was way more work than one man needed to handle alone. "I tell you what. I will get you someone to come help you so that you don't kill yourself in here." I suggested. He looked around the large stable with a smile and said "Thank you Cody but if it's all the same to you I'd rather do it alone. Being in here alone with the horses, kind of helps me get through the day. But if you insist, then that's fine." I agreed to allow him to work the stable alone considering he was still fairly new and didn't really know many of the others. I knew that he would need some time alone to process what was going on in his life. He agreed that some help would be necessary once he had things in order. I let him know that if he ever needed anything even just to talk that I was always available for him and not to hesitate to ask. Then I left him alone to do his job as he wished.

Chapter 6
Who In The Hell Is Preston

Nearly four days had passed and Ron still hadn't made it back to the ranch. We managed to get a lot of the work done around the ranch while he was gone. The field was finally plowed for the crops and things were starting to shape up nicely. Things had been pretty much quiet, with the exception of the new whitestock. He was not taking his new role of a slave so well and I didn't expect him to. Even Jacob had seemed to submit to the sting of Moses' whip. His submission was key in the others following suit. It was no easy task. It took several lashes to his backside before he was finally broken. Even with Jacob submitting to their new life, it wasn't until Moses and Jacob's son Travis came walking up to the house that I knew they all had accepted their new slave status. Bella and I were enjoying a warm Sunday afternoon on the porch when they came to see us with important information. Moses walked up onto the porch and left Travis down in the yard waiting. He said, "Good afternoon Cody…Bella. I sho hate to bother you while you's enjoying this fine afternoon but master Travis…I mean, Travis has something I think you might need to hear." Curious to know what the young whitestock could possibly have to say that I needed to hear I asked, "What is it?" Moses looked back at Travis and motioned for him to come onto the porch with us then said, "I'm going to let him tell you." Travis slowly walked up the first couple of steps then stopped and slowly took his big floppy hat off. He balled the hat up with both hands and held it closely to his chest. His mannerisms were a clear indication that he and the others were beginning to mimic the behaviors of the former slaves they had overseen for years. Even the clothes on his back that were once clean and presentable were now filthy like a common slave's. He held his head down and began to speak. Moses looked back at the trembling youngster and shouted, "Come on up closer so that master Cody and Ms. Bella can hear what you're saying there boy. Come on now! Don't get hush mouth now. Go on and tell them what you told me." Nervously, with his eyes looking down at his feet, he crept up two more steps until he was one step lower than Moses. He stood in front of us and began to stutter. "Spit it out! They don't have all day to wait on you!" Moses yelled. Travis began to tremble even more at the sound of Moses' rough delivery. "Well sir..." he started then paused as though he was going to change his mind and not talk. He looked up at Moses and saw the look on his face then quickly realized that would be a bad idea. He put his head back down then said, "It's Preston. He had everyone up all night getting their hopes up about how his business partner would come looking for him if he doesn't show up at their meeting place tomorrow. According to him they're supposed to be meeting up at some place called Hollow Hills." Bella and I asked the same question at the same time, "Who in the hell is Preston?" Travis looked up at us and said, "He's the new guy. He kept telling everyone about how his partner was a nigger killing machine." Before he could speak another word, Moses backhanded him in the mouth with a vicious left. The blow forced Travis to fall backwards down the steps. He rolled all the way to the bottom of the steps. Moses trotted down the steps and grabbed Travis by the back of his collar and lifted him off of the ground to his feet. Travis began to apologize with his hands raised to protect himself from another possible blow from Moses. "You better watch your mouth whitestock." Moses screamed at Travis. Tears were pouring down Travis' face as he tried to gather himself. "I'm sorry. Old habits die hard." Travis exclaimed. "You'll die even harder if you can't get it right. You best to find a way to forget the word 'nigger' or else." Moses appropriately responded.

Travis quickly remembered his new place and finished telling us about this new whitestock named Preston. He told us all about how Preston was bragging that he and his partner were planning to rob some wagon carrying money to a bank in town. He was afraid that his dad was beginning to get his hopes up about joining Preston and his partner. He felt that if his dad attempted to join Preston that neither of them would escape alive...and he was right. I had Moses to take Travis back to rejoin the others before they started to wonder where he was. I didn't want to alert any of the other whitestocks that we knew about the information before Bella and I could come up with a plan. I spent most of the day thinking of how to use this information to our advantage. It wasn't until sometime before supper that an idea came to me. The only problem was that I didn't have a clue as to where Hollow Hills was. That was the missing key to my plan being a success. I was going to have to get the location from Preston and I knew he was not going to give it up without forcing it out of him. After supper I walked over to the workers' quarters to see Moses. He and a group of the men were all sitting outside in a circle laughing and talking amongst themselves. When I walked up everyone greeted me with huge smiles and waves. I motioned for Moses to step away from the group so that I could have a quick word with him. I told Moses to gather everyone including all of the whitestock and wait for me in front of the big house.

The crowd was full of curiosity and chatter. The energy was extremely high for both blacks and whites. Once everyone was in place and waiting,

Bella stepped out on the porch then took a seat in one of the chairs. The crowd quickly went from a loud rumble to nearly a hush. I walked out onto the porch and stood at the top of the stairs looking out into the crowd with a smirk and said "I know that none of you ever thought that such a day would ever come. To be honest neither did I, yet here we are. As for you whitestock assholes, take a look around at all of the black faces that you once ruled over then look at yourselves. The roles have been REVERSED! You are now living the lives that they once were FORCED to live; a life of humiliation, disrespect, PAIN and suffering. For centuries you have beaten, raped and DESTROYED our people for your personal gain." At that moment I noticed the crowd was separated by more than just the colors of their skins. They were also separated by the expressions on their faces. The black faces had looks of anxiousness while the white faces held looks of fear and concern. I stepped down from the porch and stopped a few steps away from the ground. I looked out into the crowd and said, "It's been brought to my attention that there's been talk about escaping. You got big dreams about some so called 'nigger killer' coming to rescue you some day and things going back to the way they used to be." Then I walked on down to where the whitestocks were standing. I walked up face to face with Preston and said aloud, "Ain't that right Mr. Preston?" His mouth and eyes all flew wide open at the same time. He began to look around at the other whitestock and yelled "Which one of you bastards went running ya mouth to this nigger?" All of them looked just as shocked as he did…except for Travis. He was the only one of them hanging his head trying to avoid eye contact with anyone, especially Preston. His effort didn't go unnoticed by Preston. He spotted the guilt in Travis' face almost immediately after surveying the faces of the others. Soon it became obvious to them all. "It was youuu! You're the one!" Preston snarled at Travis. Jacob quickly spun around to face his son with a terrible look of disgust. "Son, how could you? You chose them over this good white man? What kind of white man are you?" Jacob yelled at Travis. The rest of the whitestocks were equally disappointed in his betrayal. Preston turned to Jacob and said, "It's all your fault for raising a nigger loving PUSSY! You must be pussy too!" Jacob turned redder than hot coals. He and Preston started towards one another when the sound of Bella cocking her rifle on the porch froze them in their tracks as well as hushing the mumbling crowd.

I slowly started circling Preston and advised, "Now if I were you, I wouldn't even say another word unless it was the directions to this Hollow Hills place." When I got back around face-to-face with him, I stopped. Again, he looked shocked that I knew about Hollow Hills. He looked me dead in my eyes then gritted his teeth and growled, "I ain't telling you NOTHING!" I turned and took a couple of steps away from him then turned back to him and said, "That's where you're wrong. Not only will you tell me how to get there, but you will tell me everything you know about this money and your nigger killing partner. Because if there's one thing I hate more than being called a nigger, it's so called nigger killers. So, you will tell me and you will tell me TONIGHT!" I placed my fingers between my lips and let out an ear-piercing whistle just the way Red Bear taught me when I was growing up. In a matter of seconds Charles came riding his horse from around the side of the house leading four more horses from the stables. I looked over at Moses and said, "Hold him!" Before Preston knew what hit him, Moses was on his back with both of his arm locked behind him. He struggled a bit but quickly realized he was no match against a man as big as Moses. I walked over to Charles and he handed me five lassos that I asked him to bring along with the horses when I called for him. I walked over to Preston with the ropes and said "You see Mr. Preston, I grew up with the Shawnee Indians as a young man. I learned a lot from them. One of the things was the art of torture." I kneeled down and put one lasso around each of his ankles then stood to face him again. I looked him in the eyes and said, "Now I'm going to give you ONE more chance to tell me how to get to Hickory Hill and anything else that I want to know." He looked me in the eye again and screamed in my face, "FUCK YOU!" I laughed and said "Nah. There won't be any fucking me. You're the only one fucked tonight my friend." Then I placed one lasso around each of his wrists. The fifth lasso I placed around his neck. Then I ordered four of my men to each take the ends of the lassos and get on one of the four horses Charles brought with him. I made sure that Moses held onto him tightly until each of the men tied their end of the lasso to their saddle horn as I instructed.

I ordered my men to have their horses to slowly walk forward until Preston's body was completely held off of the ground by the stretched out ropes. Charles manned the lasso around Preston's neck. I allowed Charles to give Preston just enough slack for him to barely speak. "You can't do this to me. This is insane!" Preston argued as he gasped for air. I walked over to his suspended body and leaned over him and said "Now I'm not playing with you. Each time that I snap my fingers my guys are going to slowly pull your ass apart taking two steps at a time." I snapped my fingers and the four with his legs and arms tied to them moved forward two steps with their horses to tighten their ropes and to stretch his limbs out even more. His agonizing screams echoed through the fields for no one but us and nature to hear him. I looked down at him and said, "I refuse to keep asking you over and over." Then I snapped my fingers again and my men didn't hesitate to walk their horses two more steps forward. Again Preston screamed out even louder than the first. Still he refused to speak. Again, I snapped and again the horses took two steps. "Ok! I'll talk." Preston screamed. Gasping for even more air he added "But first you have to put me down. Then I'll talk." I snapped my fingers again and again my men moved forward as ordered. I snapped them once more and Preston's screams graduated to full blown crying. "I said I'll talk. You don't have to do this." Preston pleaded. Again, I snapped my fingers. It was then that you could hear his arm bones dislocating from his shoulders and his legs detaching from his hip bones. All of the women both black and white simultaneously buried their faces in the chest of the closest man that wasn't too afraid to watch. I never took my eyes off of his eyes nor changed my facial expression. I raised my hand once again to snap my fingers and he began to tell me everything from directions to Hollow Hills to his partners name and description. His slobbering words provided everything that I needed to know. When he finished, he begged with drool streaming from his mouth "PLEASE PUT ME DOWN! PLEASE! I told you everything that I know. I'm in pain. I can't take no more!" I continued to stare down at him. I pulled out the poster that I had folded up in my back pocket and showed it to him. I placed it on his chest and said "Remember her? She couldn't take anymore either." Then I walked away from him snapping my fingers over and over. Each time that I snapped the horses would move until Preston's right leg came completely off. His left arm was next, followed by his right arm, leaving only his head and left leg which was barely attached by then. The blood from his torn limbs poured all over the ground. Preston yelled and screamed until he passed out. Many in the crowd threw up everywhere at the sight of his ripped apart body. Before his last limb could break off, I yelled "STOP!" I walked over to Preston and gave him a couple of slaps across the face to bring him conscious again. He was groggy and still suspended in the air. He opened his eyes and I said to him, "I told you that you would talk. Now I'll cut you a loose." I walked over to the rope around his ankle then pulled out my knife. I cut the rope and his leg fell to the ground. I walked back over to look him in his eyes. "Now you're going on your final ride." I raised my hand again and gave one last snap. Charles took off on his horse as fast as he could with the rope still tied around Preston's neck. His body bounced and tumbled across the rugged field like a sack of potatoes. You could hear his cries as the horse reached top speed until Preston's head snapped off like an apple picked from a tree. Then I walked back into the house with Bella following behind me totting her gun.

Chapter 7
Guess Who's Coming To Dinner

Things around the ranch were pretty quiet among the whitestock for awhile. No one was in any hurry to be ripped apart like Preston. They were also not letting up on giving Travis the cold shoulder. To make matters worse I made Travis a servant in my house so that he didn't have to work in the field, just to piss off the other whitestock. The sight of him in clean clothes and standing next to Bella and I on the porch with his silver serving tray made their blood boil. I even think it pissed Jacob off more than actually being a slave himself. No one was more taken aback to see him as a servant than Ron when he finally came riding up one afternoon. Bella and I were sitting on the porch in our rocking chairs enjoying a midday drink of sweet tea and whiskey when Ron rode up in his wagon. I was surprised to see that he wasn't alone. Sitting next to him on the wagon was a dark haired older white woman. She looked to be slightly younger than Ron but quite a bit older than Bella and I. Bella and I left Travis on the porch while we stepped down to greet Ron and his lady friend. "What the hell is going on here?" Ron asked pointing back to the porch at Travis. "I could ask you the same thing" I responded. I was somewhat concerned about her presence considering she didn't appear to be new whitestock. That is, until I heard Bella say out of the blue "Honee…Bee." I immediately whipped around at Bella shocked at her outburst. "Bella…Rose. It's good to see you again. How…in the hell…are YOU?" the lady responded then the two hugged and rocked back and forth. Then the two ladies walked off arm and arm leaving us at the wagon. The lady leaned over and whispered something to Bella then looked back at us with a smile. Bella turned her head back at us smiling and I heard her tell the lady "Yeah that's my Cody." They giggled and the lady responded, "He's handsome." They kept walking to the house. Ron asked, "So now that you've met Honee, you mind telling me why in the hell is he on the porch dressed like that?" I laughed and said "First of all, I haven't met Honee YET. And I'll explain about

Travis over dinner AFTER I officially meet Ms. Honee."

Ron and Honee went straight to his room once we got their bags inside of the house. They stayed in there for hours making noises that made my skin crawl. I didn't know old people could go for so long. I eventually decided to just go have a seat on the porch while Bella and Travis prepared dinner. I wasn't out there very long before Ron and Honee both finally came out and joined me. Honee took a seat in the rocking chair that Bella normally sat in and I stood to allow Ron to have my seat. God knows he looked as though he needed it. He was clearly winded and her hair was a bit shuffled. Ron took his seat and reached inside of his vest then pulled out a flask from his inside pocket. He uncapped the flask and took a quick sip. "Aaaaagh…well earned," he said then passed the flask to Honee. She took the flask and put it to her lips then threw her head back. She wiped the drippings from her mouth with the sleeve of her dress. She passed the flask to me and I turned it up the same way that she did but had to back off of it a lot quicker than Honee. I shook my head and asked, "What in the HELL is this?" The two of them had a good laugh at my expense. Ron sat up in his seat then blurted out "That's some of Virginia's finest hooch brewed in the mountains. It's also some of the strongest." Honee began to rock in her chair then proudly said, "That comes from my brothers' still. It's a family recipe passed on for generations sweetie. It doesn't get any better than this right here sugar." Ron smiled equally as proud and announced, "Her family is well known for their spirits around these parts." I nodded my head and sarcastically questioned "So is that how you two met?" Ron shook his head no then added "Don't be silly. Honee and I go way back. We first met when we were teenagers. She was fifteen and I was nineteen. Every other summer my parents would send my siblings and me to spend a couple of weeks here with my aunt. As you know I never cared for the visits here with the way they treated the slaves and all of that foolishness. Honee was the only person that seemed to share my disdain for the business. Although her family could not afford to own any, they strongly opposed slavery as she did. As much as they disliked slavery, they disliked slave owners themselves even more than the business. My aunt did not approve of me seeing her on the count of her family not being as financially stable. Her family in turn felt that I was only after one thing because I came from money. Well we didn't let that stop us. We would find ways to meet up. One of our favorite meeting places was Miller's Pond on the other side of the woods about a mile and a half from here. Old man Miller used to let us help him feed his livestock. That's where I first saw her. She had been going over there to help out just to earn a little extra money for her family. I was down visiting and stumbled across the pond one day while I was out walking. I decided that the next day I'd come back and do a little fishing while everyone else was back at the house. Well I was in the middle of trying to pull in a fish when I heard the loud squeaky voice scream 'you put that fish right back in that water'. She startled me so badly that I threw my pole straight in the air and the fish took off with my pole and all. I turned around and there stood this scrawny little thing with her hands on her hips. I didn't know what to do but then she burst out laughing and pointing at me. She was the cutest thing that I'd ever seen. We spent the rest of the day talking and the rest was history."

Honee laughed then started rocking in her chair and said, "Yeah but there's a lot of memories and stories in that history. I've been with Ron through the good and the bad. Even when he told Carolyn that he was going to search for his daughter Bella, she couldn't accept it." She reached over and patted Ron's hand and added "But we found her together." Ron's eyebrows raised and my jaw dropped. The looks on our faces was all Honee needed to know that neither of us were expecting that blow. Honee's jaw dropped as well. She turned to Ron and said, "Ronnie tell me you haven't been keeping this a secret from her all of these years." Slowly Ron lowered his head and nodded his head yes. "Oh my God Ronnie, why haven't you told that poor child by now? That's been over ten years," Honee continued. By then I had begun to pace back and forth trying to wrap my mind around what I just heard. I was just as confused as Honee as to why he hadn't told Bella. I stopped pacing and stood in front of Ron then said, "So all along you've been lying to all of us, not to mention how Bella's going to feel when she finds out." Ron jumped to his feet and grabbed both of my arms begging "PLEASE! Don't tell her. She mustn't know…at least not now, not yet. I just need a little more time. I promise, I'm going to tell her. But I have some things that I have to do first." That's when Honee stood and said, "Time? How much more time do you need darling? The woman has gone through her entire life not knowing who her father was and he was right next to her the whole time. You've had more than enough time. You need to tell her or I will." Honee was so upset that she stomped off and went back into the house. "What in the hell is she talking about Ron?" I demanded. Ron looked back at the front door then sat back down in the rocking chair and began to shake his head. He looked up at me then said, "You might want to sit down for this." I shook my head no and answered, "I'd rather stand if it's alright with you." He lowered his head again and said "Very well then. Stand if you must but I don't guess it matters if you're standing or sitting but what Honee said about me being Bella's father is true. I never meant for this to go on for so long, but I could never find the right words, the right time nor the courage to tell her. For years I've wanted nothing more than to tell her the truth." My knees felt weak and I decided to take that seat after all. "But how? How could you be her father when for so long she thought her master was her dad?" I desperately asked. He took a deep breath then said, "My full name is Ronald Langford Frost." For a moment I was perplexed because the name Frost sounded familiar. Then it hit me like a raging bull. I asked "Frost? Isn't that the…" but before I could get it out Ron interrupted me with "Yes…it's the last name of Bella's first master. Theodore Frost was my older brother. Teddy was what we called him within the family. When our father became ill I traveled to his home to deliver the news. It had been awhile since I had seen him because of my disapproval of slavery. Nevertheless, I was still compelled to inform him of just how sick our father had become. The day that I arrived, Teddy had just returned from the slave auction with three new slaves he'd purchased, two young males and one female. The female was Bella's mother. Her name was Summer…Summer Rose. Like Bella, she was mixed as well but Summer's mother was white and her father was a slave. When Bella's mother was born looking less than white, the husband went into a fit of rage and killed his wife and the slave. He didn't have the heart to kill a baby, so he sold Bella's mother into a life of slavery. One of the men that Teddy purchased along with Summer rebelled and Teddy ordered him to be whipped as the other two were forced to watch as a means of intimidation. When I rode up on my horse I found Teddy with them in the front yard. 'Again!' he yelled for his overseer to issue another flesh ripping lash from his whip. 'ENOUGH!' I screamed. I jumped off of my horse and rushed over to the man. He was shaking like crazy and crying like a child. It was horrible. His hands and feet were tied around a large tree in the front yard so that he couldn't escape the punishment. I covered the man with my body to prevent the whip happy overseer from delivering anymore lashes. 'Get out of the way you fool.' Teddy screamed at me but I refused. Finally, Teddy sent the overseer away and I cut the ropes to release the poor slave. He fell to the ground sobbing. The three of them were then taken away to their quarters. As they walked away the young woman continued to look back at me as though she wanted me to come save her too. If only I could have, I would have saved them all."

It was clear that Ron was becoming emotional, but he continued. He said "Originally I had planned to deliver the news about father and leave out the next day. As much as I despised being there, I couldn't bring myself to leave out so fast. The next day I went out to the field to find the new woman while Teddy and the rest of his family went into town. I knew that if I took her from the field that the overseers would inform Teddy and could possibly get her in some sort of trouble. So, I just watched her from afar. I knew that Teddy and the others would be gone for awhile. I was determined to see her. When the field work was done for the day, I found her sitting under a tree with a group of other female slaves. The sun was beginning to set and a cool breeze was blowing through her long straight hair. I stopped a few feet away from the tree and motioned for her to come to me. At first she was a bit apprehensive which was understandable considering she didn't know me or my intentions but she came anyway. I was glad that she did. She was even more beautiful up close than I realized. We spent the next couple of hours talking. I discovered that not only was she beautiful but that she was extremely smart as well. To make a long story short, I ended up staying for nearly a week. I had gained not only her trust but feelings as well. I began to make up excuses to visit Teddy just so that I could see Summer. It didn't take long for Teddy to figure out what I was doing but he never said anything until I showed up unexpectedly at his home one day. Teddy was away on business when I arrived. It had been a few months since I had been to see her and couldn't get her off of my mind. When I got there, I could hear the bone chilling sounds of a whip's cracking sound in the air and the soul wrenching pleas for mercy of a woman coming from behind the big house. I jumped off of my horse and rushed to the back. Twice more the whip cracked and twice more she screamed louder than the last. When I got around to the back, I found Teddy's wife standing next to three men. I looked around for a victim but didn't see anyone. Just then one of the guys reached back with a whip and came down with a lightning fast lash to the ground. Again, the sound of a woman's cry rang out but I still couldn't see her. I ran over as fast as I could pushing and forcing my way through the four of them to see what was going on. When I finally got through, I found my beautiful Summer lying on the ground face down. Her hands and feet were stretched out and tied down with stakes in the ground. The back of her dress was split open to expose her back for the whip to make direct contact. I dropped to my knees to let her know that I was there and that she was safe. Her face and hair were covered in dirt, sweat and tears. She was petrified. Her eyes were frozen wide open in a state of shock. I stood up and drew my pistol then blew a hole in the shoulder of the bastard holding the whip. He dropped the whip and grabbed his shoulder then fell to the ground. I cocked the gun and aimed it at the next man. My sister-in-law raised her hands for me to stop then jumped in front of the guy. She begged me not to shoot. I made the two fellas untie Summer and get her to her feet. That's when I really became outraged. I looked down at the ground and realized there was a huge hole dug out. It was for Summer to lay her impregnated belly in while she received her lashes. I looked at the hole then at Summer's belly several times.

When Teddy came home he was pissed of course. I later found out that Summer was receiving her beating because she was accused of being too lazy in the field. Even though Teddy was pissed, I made him promise that nothing like that would happen to her again or else I would come back to kill every worker he had. Teddy agreed under the condition that I stayed away from his home so often and unexpected. We lost our father a few weeks later after that. Then my wife became pregnant as well. I very well couldn't leave her alone to just to check up on a woman that I was not even supposed to be involved with in the first place. Months went by and my wife Carolyn gave birth to our stillborn daughter. It devastated us both but Carolyn was never the same afterwards. She was in a state of depression for months until she discovered she was pregnant once again. Months went by and again another stillborn girl. She felt even more crushed and betrayed by God. It almost ruined our marriage. Meanwhile, I had missed the birth of Bella and Carolyn was getting no better. Eventually months turned to years and I never went back but I thought about Summer every day. I just couldn't bring myself to leave Carolyn alone in that state. I was torn between a rock and a hard place. By the time Carolyn began to come around I finally got a chance to visit but Bella was no baby anymore. She was about five or six years old. I made Teddy promise to treat her well and to educate her as I would. He kept his word on up until the day Summer was killed. By the time I found out about what happened to her, Bella had been gone for over two years. Teddy refused to tell me where she was and threatened to tell my wife if I brought any harm to anymore of his workers. It wasn't until Teddy was on his death bed that he finally told me who he sold Bella to. He knew that I loved my child and didn't want to leave this world without making that last amends. I searched for Bella for months after Teddy passed but I couldn't find her anywhere. Carolyn and I had grown so far apart that I no longer desired to stay with her. It wasn't the depression that made me leave. I just fell out of love. So, I left on a mission to find my daughter. I turned to the one person that always had my back to help me look for her and that was Honee. Honee had family and connections everywhere. Eventually we found her and Honee went back home. You pretty much know the rest from there." Before I could say a word, Bella stepped out onto the porch and said, "Dinner is ready you two." Then she walked back inside. Ron got up and followed her while I was stuck in my seat with my mouth open.

Chapter 8
Back To The Business

After dinner Bella called it an early night and went to bed. Honee was still upset with Ron so she also went to bed not long after dinner. Ron and I allowed the ladies to get their rest without any argument from either of us. I found myself in my new favorite spot, the rocking chair on the porch. I took one chair and Ron of course took the other one. There was an awkward silence for a moment until Ron broke it with, "That was really smart making Travis a servant. I'm sure it's caused some problems with the other whitestock." He glanced over at me to see for a response and quickly realized he wasn't getting one. He turned his focus back to the open field and sighed. Again, we shared another silent moment, but he didn't let that stop him. Again, he broke the silence. He glanced back at me then to the field and said, "I take it you got the whole pull a man apart from your time growing up with the Shawnee Indians huh? I bet that put some fear in the..." Before he could continue, I had to interrupt him. "She's your DAUGHTER!" I growled in a low tone and gritting my teeth without even turning my head. He quickly turned to face me. "Let me explain" he pleaded. Again, I refused to look at him. "What kind of man would have his own daughter to rob and kill for him?" I continued but still trying not to be too loud. I didn't want Bella to hear us. Although I wanted her to know the truth, I didn't want her to find out that way. I was so furious that I couldn't bring myself to even look at him until he quickly hopped to his feet and stepped directly in front of me. As quickly as he was to his feet I was up on my feet as well. Had he been twenty years younger I would have knocked him on his ass. Even though I was way taller and stronger than him he didn't back down. He turned redder than an apple and said, "Look a here god damn it! I love Bella with all of my heart. I have tried to tell her several times. Do you think it's been easy for me to live a life of a lie for so many years? Hell no! Before my wife got pregnant, I was planning to buy Bella and Summer's freedom from my brother then leave my wife. But once I found out that she was pregnant there was no way that I could leave her. Then when she lost the babies, she became cold and distant. It was like she was trying to drive me away. When I decided that I had enough, I also decided to get Summer and Bella." The look on his face slowly went from anger to hurt as he lowered his head and turned away from me. He placed his hands on the banister of the porch then raised his head and said, "By then Summer was gone and

Bella was too. I checked with the family my brother sold Bella to but of course she was gone. She had killed off the other family that bought her and she was living in the shadows after that. She was killing and doing whatever it took to survive when I met her. I tried to stop her when I first found her, but she killed a man the night I met her."

His words were bone-chilling and grabbed my attention even more. I sat back down and asked, "What happened?" Ron took his seat and rocked back and forth in the chair a couple of times then said "Well I had word that she may have been headed up north, so I followed her. Her trail went cold the farther north I traveled. I turned to my last resort, Honee. I told Honee everything and she just so happened to be good friends with a negro woman that was helping other negroes to escape to freedom up north. She led me damn near right to her. When I found Bella, she was being harassed by a saloon owner for eating out of the garbage behind his saloon. I convinced the owner to spare her life. The saloon owner walked back inside and let us leave without calling the sheriff but what we didn't know was that there was a man across the street watching the whole thing. He took it upon himself to approach us and take matters in his own hands. He started shouting about how I was a nigger lover and deserved to hang next to Bella. Well as you can imagine, I didn't take too kindly to his words, but I tried to ignore him so that we could get the hell out of there. Bella on the other hand was not so willing to turn the other cheek nor act as if she didn't hear him as I was doing. The more he screamed and yelled the more agitated Bella became. He was approaching from our right and Bella was between the two of us. I grabbed her hand to get her to hurry along with me. That's when the guy takes off in a slow trot to catch up with us. He said something about her being an animal or some shit and that's when his trot and his life came to an end. Before I knew what was happening Bella had shot the man twice in the chest. He grabbed his chest then dropped to the ground face first. She wanted to go put more holes in him, but I pulled her back. I knew that those shots were going to eventually bring people out to see what happened. We ran to my cart and high tailed it out of there just in time. Had we gotten caught, we definitely would have hung together. Later on I asked why didn't she shoot the saloon owner if she had a gun. She said, 'if I had killed him then the saloon would have closed and I wouldn't have had anywhere to get food.' Then I asked, why kill the other man and she simply said, 'he didn't own a saloon.' I knew then that I had to get her out of town and further north. She had been through so much that I just couldn't bring myself to tell her that I was her father. I tried plenty of times but the more time we spent together the closer we became. Her trust in white people was already gone. I didn't want to give her a reason to put me in the same category as the others. I took her to stay with Honee and her family for a few months until I could put an end to my marriage. Honee's father took her in with the rest of their family and treated her as so. It was just what she needed to see that all white men weren't evil. Once my divorce was finalized, I returned to Honee's to get Bella. It's been the two of us, every since. Then you came along. Now I feel a little more comfortable about dying knowing that she has a man like you to look after her. You were the answer to the question of when will I tell her."

Again, his words gripped me like a vice. The two of us sat in our chairs in silence for a moment. I was still trying to wrap my mind around everything Ron just told me. I thought that he may have been thinking about it as well. Then he said, "I found out what I needed while I was in town." I turned and asked, "What did you find out?" He reached inside of his vest pocket and pulled out his trusty liquor flask. He took a sip then passed it to me. He wiped his mouth with his hand and said,

"Do you remember the Matthews brothers I told you about, Harry and Terry?" I took a sip and nodded my head yes. I passed the flask back to Ron and asked, "What about them?" Ron tucked his flask back in his vest pocket and said "Well every year they normally have a huge birthday party for themselves. From the look on your face I obviously failed to mention, they're twins." He was right, I was a bit confused. "Go on." I said. He smirked then replied "Anyway, I had the dates wrong. The party is in two weeks. It's the perfect opportunity to have them in the same place at the same time. That will be easier than making two attempts to grab them. All we have to do is get into the party and grab them without anyone seeing us. And I know just how to do it." Two weeks wasn't a very long time, but we had nothing to lose. If we pulled this off it would be huge. "So how do you plan to get into the party?" I asked. He smiled and said "Well that's where Honee comes in. The twins are notorious drinkers and gamblers.

Honee's family has a hand in both and a disliking for the twins. They not only have identical features they also have identical bad luck. They have been known to owe way more than they could pay. Right now they're in debt to her family for a little over ten thousand dollars and they're not too pleased with them right now. So, our timing couldn't be better. Honee and I are going to meet with her brothers in a couple of days to discuss collecting on their debts. But I'm curious to know what you plan to do about Preston's friend and the money that's coming." I stroked my beard stubble and said "Oh I have a plan for him. I'm leaving early in the morning with Moses and Jordan to meet him where he was supposed to meet Preston." Ron's eyes grew big with excitement then said "I think I'll tag along. Besides, Honee's not going to be so forgiving any time soon."

Chapter 9
The Mission

The next morning the four of us hit the trail headed for Hollow Hills. It took nearly three hours to reach our destination. It was a beautiful undeveloped area with big green hills for miles. It was called Hollow Hills because most of the hills had caves in them. We followed Preston's directions and they led us straight to their little secret hideout. The hideout was a cave in a large hill set low in the valley about a mile off from the main trail. It was hidden perfectly and easy to miss for an unsuspected looker. We reached the top of a small cliff that allowed us to look down over and across straight to their hideout. It was easy to recognize from Preston's description. There was one large boulder on each side of the entrance just as he described. There was also a horse tied down right outside of the entrance which confirmed that we had the right location. "What's the plan now boss?" Jordan asked. I looked over to him and said "Well Jordan according to Preston the money should have come through sometime between late last night and early this morning. Now the way I see it Preston's partner Frank, the 'Nigger Killer' had no choice but to take the stagecoach alone once he realized Preston wasn't coming." That's when it all started to make sense to everyone else. Moses smiled and said, "That means he's held up in that cave with an ass load of money and by himself. He's not going to wait on Preston much longer before he hightails it out of there before the bank sends someone looking their money. Now we don't have to hang for robbing a bank's stagecoach and no one will be looking for us after we take the money from Frank's dead ass." I placed my hand on Moses' shoulder and said, "That's right and we can split the money evenly between me, you and Jordan." Jordan instantly became concerned that I didn't mention Ron's name. "What about Mr. Ron?" he asked. "Oooh don't worry about me kid.

I'm just along for the fun of it." Ron responded with a chuckle. Jordan was wowed at Ron's lack of interest in the money. Jordan scratched his head then said, "I don't think I've ever met a white man that didn't want to get more money." Ron smiled and said "It's not always about the money kid. But if we don't get down here to the money then it's not going to even matter. So, let's get on down here a pay old Frank a visit before the trail is swarming with bounty hunters." Then he headed down the steep drop off and we all followed.

We knew that we couldn't just ride down and get picked off like bottles on a fence post for target practice. We decided to flank the entrance from the right and surprise him. We tied our horses to a couple of large bushes several feet from the entrance. We slowly approached the large hill then quickly rushed to the side of the cave entrance with our backs against the moss-covered outer wall of the hill. We inched our way step by step with me leading and Moses right behind me then Jordan with Ron pulling up the rear. I crouched down to one knee then peeped my head around the huge rock to check for Frank's location inside. There he was, Frank the "Nigger Killer." He was sitting on a big stone with his back to the entrance. I sent Moses and Jordan to run to the other side to hide behind the other boulder across the entrance. They barely made to the other side without him seeing them, but he still heard their footsteps. He whipped around with his pistol drawn and shouted, "Who's there?" Just then out of nowhere a jackrabbit scurried across the ground in front of the cave relieving him of any suspicions. The rabbit went about his way and Frank holstered his pistol then turned back around with his back to the entrance. That's when the four of us stepped in front of the entrance and drew our pistols. The sounds of our footsteps and guns whipping out of our holsters put an immediate halt to what he was doing. He was in the middle of transferring the money from the bank bags to his own saddlebags. Slowly he raised both of his hands with the saddlebag in his left and a fistful of money in his right hand. He opened his hands and both the bag and the money fell to the ground. "Pick it up and finish what you were doing or else." I told him. "Or else what? Fuck you!" he responded in a deep voice. His cockiness pissed me off. "Or else you won't even see it coming" I snarled back. Lucky for him it was enough to convince him that it was in his best interest to do as I said or die.

Once he finished stuffing both sides of two large saddlebags full of money, he angrily said "That's all of it. Now who in the hell are you?" My eyes lowered and a smile formed on my face. I answered, "Me? Well I'm the 'Nigger Killer's Killer." He looked extremely lost, so I helped bring him up to speed. I advised him "According to your late partner Preston, you're quite the nigger killing machine. Let him tell it there ain't a nigger alive that you wouldn't or couldn't kill if you chose to do so." He tilted his head and asked

"What do you mean…late? Where's Preston?" He began to reach for his gun again until the four of us cocked our guns. He knew that he didn't stand a chance, so he rethought his decision and slowly lowered his hand to his side. He may have been crazy, but he was no fool. I walked just inside of the entrance of the cave and took a glance around. It was pretty deeper and wider than I imagined once I got inside. I have to give it to them; they had pretty much everything that you would need to camp out for a few days. They even had two small homemade beds for each of themselves. I uncocked my gun then twirled it around with my finger and placed it back in my holster. I walked up closer to him but not too close, just close enough to see into his eyes. They were cold and empty just as I would expect any demon to look. I said, "Your friend Preston had the unfortunate luck of crossing the paths of my good friends over there. He was then brought to my ranch to perform manual labor until he…well let's just say he fell apart." There was a light chuckle from everyone except for Frank of course. I pulled a bullet from my gun belt and looked at it then back at Frank and said, "I tell you what. I'll give you a chance that I didn't give ole Frank. If you can catch two bullets in a row with your hand, I'll let you live." He giggled and said, "Shiiiit that's nothing. Go ahead. I can catch, you son of a bitch." I smiled and quickly tossed the bullet to him as fast as I could. Sure enough, he caught it in his hand and held it up with a snaggletooth smile. The few teeth that he did have were just as dirty and nasty as his beard looked. I pulled out another bullet and said, "I see you're pretty quick huh?" He smirked and nodded his head then threw the bullet to the ground. He said "You damn right I am. I'm faster than any nigger. Even you! So, come on! I bet I catch the next one too." It turned out that he was right. He did catch the next one, only it wasn't in his hand. It was in his gut and I didn't throw it with my hand. I shot it from my gun before he even knew what happened. He grabbed his stomach with both hands then dropped to his knees. The blood was pouring from him like a waterfall. He looked down at his stomach then back up at me and said, "You said you wouldn't kill me. You lied to me." I walked over to him and stood over him with my pistol aimed at his forehead. I said, "I didn't lie to you. You assumed that I was going to throw you this bullet and you ain't dead…yet. But you didn't catch the bullet in your hand either, now did you?" I could see that the bullet had blown straight throw his back while he was doubled over. He managed to muster up enough strength to sit up and say, "Go to hell NIGGER!" I responded, "You first!" then I pulled the trigger. After that we wasted no time getting out of there as fast as we could.

Chapter 10
The Cat Is Out of the Bag

It took us a little longer to get back than it did to get there. It took longer because I wanted to make sure that we covered our tracks back to the ranch. I didn't want to lead anyone back to our homes. We used an old Indian trick I learned as a young man. I had everyone to tie long wide tree branches with plenty of leaves to the end of their horses' tails far down enough to drag the ground. The trailing branches swept away the hoof tracks of our horses so that no one could see which direction we left. We even took an extra mile or so out of the way just to be extra careful. We arrived back at the ranch a few hours before nightfall. We made it in just in time for supper. Bella and Honee were in the kitchen with Travis finishing whipping up a meal. Before we could get through the door good Bella came stomping full speed towards us. She stopped in front of us then slammed her hands on her hips and laid into both of us. She screamed at Ron, "How long have you known, huh? What…did you think you could keep something like this from me forever? Why would you do that?" Ron and I both just dropped our heads. Then she turned to me and said, "So you knew too?" I opened my mouth to speak and couldn't find any words that could help ease her sense of betrayal in me. I was speechless. She was so upset that she hauled off and gave me a swift smack across the face. The actual blow was nowhere near as painful as the feeling of disappointment in me that I was receiving from her. Plus, I'd seen Bella's punishing blows before and this was not one of them. Although at that moment I'd rather received one of those with hopes of being knocked unconscious rather than answer why I didn't tell that she was Ron's daughter. Ron opened his mouth to speak but was also cut short. But unlike me, he was cut short by Honee rushing out of the kitchen. She was drying her hands with a rag.

"Now hold on there Bella before you get yourself all worked up again. It's not his fault this time. I asked Ronnie not to say anything to you about it and to let me be the one to break the news to you." Honee exclaimed as she quickly embraced Bella and turned her to look her eye to eye. She held Bella by the shoulders and said with sincere compassion, "He was old darling. He lived a good life…a full life. But it was just time for him to go to heaven sweetie. We all miss my father. But he's in a better place now." Honee then pulled Bella in close to her for a big hug. Bella buried her face in Honee's shoulder to fight back the tears. Honee looked over Bella's shoulder at Ron and I mouthed "Shut up." We did just that and stood there while Honee consoled Bella. She said, "You fellas just so happened to walk in as I was telling Bella about my father passing away a few years ago. Just give her a moment. She'll be just fine." Then the two of them walked upstairs to our room and closed the door behind them. Ron and I were both relieved that Honee came in before either of us opened our mouths and let the real cat out of the bag about her being Ron's daughter.

Bella never came back out of the room even for dinner. Ron, Honee and I took to the porch after dinner. I allowed Ron and Honee to take a seat in the rocking chairs while I leaned against the porch banister. I also wanted to be facing the front door just in case Bella decided to come down to join us. I didn't want her to walk up on us talking. Ron broke the ice with "That was a close call. For a second there I thought that you had told her. I almost spilled the beans and told it on myself." I smirked and shook my head. Honee on the other hand expressed her feelings by rolling her eyes then folding her arms really hard and offering a stern, "HUMPH!" Luckily for Ron we had an unexpected visitor to draw the attention away from him for the moment. It was the wild horse that I wanted. He trotted out from the trees and stood in the opening as though he was on display. He stood there posing with the sunset behind him as his backdrop highlighting his muscular physique. His presence immediately captured my attention which in turn drew the attention of Ron and Honee when they saw me gazing out into the field. I walked off of the porch. Although he was way too far for either of us to have any concerns of the other being hurt, he almost appeared to be not just calm but inviting. I walked out into the field and stopped. We stared at one another for a moment. Then the most amazing thing happened. He started to walk towards me. He took several more steps in my direction then stopped. He raised his nose high in the air and sniffed the air a few times then slowly turned around. He looked back at me and tossed his head up and down repeatedly then trotted off a few steps. He looked back at me and did it again. Up and down his head went then he turned and galloped back towards the woods. Just then the sky got dark out of nowhere. Then there was a chest rattling sound of thunder followed by heavy rain and lightning. I stood there for a moment looking at him as he reached the edge of the tree line. He looked back at me again. I then realized that he was trying to warn me of the storm. I knew then that he was meant for me and I was meant for him. I ran back to the porch to get out of the rain. Ron and Honee were having a good hardy laugh at my expense of getting soaked. Honee stood and headed inside. Just before she walked in she stopped at the door then turned and said "If you're thinking about riding that horse you better eat a good breakfast. He's a smart one." Then she walked inside shaking her head and laughing. Ron and I sat on the porch while I dried up enough to go inside without getting the floor soaking wet as well. We sat there watching the rain fall. The sound of the drops beating down was all to be heard until Ron said, "I think I will allow you and the ladies take the trip to visit Honee's brothers without me." His decision took me by surprise. I wasn't expecting it. "Are you sure? Why the sudden change of plans?" I asked. Ron stood then pulled on his suspenders with his thumbs then dropped his and said "That's a pretty long ride and neither of them is too pleased with me right about now. I don't know about you, but I don't want to ride for hours watching what I say. That's just one way. You're going to have to stay overnight to let the horses rest then another long ride coming back. Think about it! The slightest thing could send either one of them into a fit that the devil himself couldn't stand. Yeah...I'm definitely sure. Besides, someone should probably stay here on the ranch just in case something happens. Don't stay up too late. Honee will be up early and ready to ride. Goodnight." He walked inside leaving me on the porch alone. To be honest, he was right. Even I was a bit concerned about leaving Moses and the others at the ranch alone for so long. It gave me some comfort knowing that he would be there as well.

Chapter 11
Family Ties

Sure enough, Honee was up just before sunrise and knocking at our bedroom door just like Ron said she would. To my surprise Bella was already up and half dressed herself when Honee came knocking. Bella opened the door and Honee walked in and shamelessly snatched the blanket clean off of me. Luckily for me I had my pajamas on, but I still snatched Bella's pillow up to cover up my junk. "What the hell?" I yelled but she just laughed and pointed at me. Honee stood on the side of the bed with both hands on her hips and said "Son you ain't got nothing that I ain't seen many of and many times. I've seen all shapes, sizes AND...coloooors. So, get on up and get them balls to jingling so we can get out of here." Then she walked over to where Bella was standing across the room and I quickly grabbed the blanket to cover myself even more. The two of them laughed at me while Honee helped Bella close up the back of her dress. "I'll be downstairs waiting for you two. Don't take too long I have breakfast on the table waiting on ya. You don't want to let it get too cold." Honee said as she walked back out of the room closing the door behind her and still laughing. Bella came and took a seat on the bed next to me still laughing as well. I sat up and said "Well I'm just glad to see you laughing again. After last night I wasn't sure if it was safe to come to bed. I just took a chance. But it's damn sure good to see that pretty smile of yours again." She gave me a kiss and said, "Well Honee and I talked last night when we came upstairs. She explained that you had no idea what or who I was talking about. So, I apologize for slapping you. Do you forgive me?" I smiled then she leaned in for a kiss and I said "No." That's when she pounced on top of me and straddled me. She looked down at me with an evil grin then reached underneath her and pulled out my Johnson from between the buttons of my pajamas. She spread open her dress and placed me inside of her warm love. She closed her eyes and placed both of her hands on my chest. "We don't have time for this Bella. Honee is downstairs waiting for us," I moaned. She placed her hand over my mouth and said, "Shhhhhhh! This won't take me long at all. You just lay still." She threw her head back then began to buck as though she was trying to break a horse for riding. She was right. It wasn't long before both of us were moaning and groaning until Bella collapsed on my chest. "Do you accept my apology now?" she asked softly. All I could do was smile. Needless to say, that our breakfast was cold and Honee was sitting in a kitchen chair with her legs crossed waiting on us while she finished her cup of coffee. "Well now that you've gotten that out of the way maybe you have an appetite for some cold breakfast," Honee advised with a sneaky grin then taking a sip of her coffee. Bella pranced over to Honee and gave her a hug from behind and told her, "I'm warm enough that I don't need my food to be hot." They both laughed but I didn't say a word. I just sat my ass down and tried not to look Honee in the eye while I ate my food.

We agreed that it would be best to use a wagon instead of individual horses. Bella and I rode in the back while Honee sat up front. We didn't want to raise any suspicions if we ran into someone along the way. It was a long bumpy ride, but we made it the entire way without any run-ins with any troubles. Honee stopped the wagon and announced to us, "We're here!" Bella and I climbed out of the back of the wagon and stretched our limbs. We stepped to the front of the wagon to join Honee. She was standing in front of a huge rundown looking two-story house. "Is this it? Is this where your brothers stay?" I asked disappointedly. Honee and Bella both smiled and started walking off leading the horses and wagon towards the house. They walked on ahead of me to the back of the old house and tied the horses to a tree in the back. I walked up as they were walking away from the wagon and I said to them, "It looks abandoned." They gave me more smiles then walked off as though I hadn't said a word. Instead of walking towards the house they headed farther back towards the wooded area away from the house. I looked back at the house then to them and back to the house. I realized they were not coming back, so I trotted off behind them. "Wait up. Where are you going?" I yelled out but they continued walking as though I still hadn't said a word. I hurried and caught up with them before they got too far away to see where they were going. Bella had the biggest smile that I had ever seen on her pretty face. Bella turned to Honee and said, "It's just like I remember from when I was a child."

We walked for a couple of minutes or so through thick bushes, tall grass and huge trees. Soon the trees cleared and another house appeared; a much nicer house in fact. Bella took off running for the front door and a white man in dirty overalls stepped out on the porch with a shotgun in his hands. His salt and pepper beard stretched down to the top of his stomach. He started to raise the gun and I slowly began to reach for the pistol on my hip but Honee quickly grabbed my hand. I looked down at her hand on mine then she pointed at Bella and said, "No need for that. Just watch." I looked back up and he was lowering his weapon. The man then turned around and yelled into the house "Hey Tiny come quick. Look who's here!" He leaned his shotgun against the house and headed off of the porch in a hurried shuffle. He wasn't moving very fast at all, but he was moving as fast as his old body would allow. Just as he was reaching the bottom of the three-step porch Bella was there to meet him with a huge hug. "What in tar nation are you out here yapping about?" another much larger white man said as he walked out onto the porch. He was the biggest man that I had ever seen in my life. He was so big and tall that he had to duck down when he came out of the house. "Well I'll be. Carl is that who I think it is?" he said with his hands on his hips and staring out at Bella and his brother hugging still. Bella released Carl and charged up the porch to give the other brother a big hug as well. He raised her off of her feet and spun around with her as though she was a small child. Honee and I watched the three of them exchange hugs then Honee started walking towards to house. I was stuck still amazed at just how big her brothers were, especially Tiny. Honee looked back at me and said "Well don't just stand there. Come on up and meet my brothers. They don't bite, unless you mess with me, Bella or their money." She waved her hand for me to follow then turned back around and continued walking to the house. "What about me? I'm the one that brought her here. Don't I get no love?" Honee yelled out to her brothers. I followed Honee to join everyone else at the house. There weren't too many men that I ever had to look up to once I became grown myself. But there I was, face to face with not one but two men that I had to slightly tilt my head back to see them eye to eye. When Honee introduced me to them and I shook their hands. Carl's hands were about the same size as mine but Tiny's hand wrapped around mine like I was a baby. He pulled me in close with a quick snatch and put his large arm around my shoulder then pointed at Bella and said with a smile, "That right there is my family. You see that smile on her face? As long as you can keep a smile on her face like that right there, then you're family too. BUT…if you ever cross her and hurt her in anyway, then there ain't nowhere on God's green earth that you can hide from us. You got that?" I smiled back and answered, "I appreciate you welcoming me to your family BUT, first of all, Bella is my lady and I love her. I would never do anything to hurt her. But do you want to know something more important than that?" He grinned and said, "What's that?" That's when I stopped smiling and said, "If you ever threaten me again, make damn sure that you are ready to put in some work!" Then he looked down at his stomach where he could feel the sharp point of my hunting knife firmly pressed against his belly. When he looked back up at me, I had an even bigger smile than before. He looked at his brother then to Bella and Honee. He looked back at me and said, "Oh I like you!" Without warning he started laughing and bear hugged me then lifted me off of the ground with no regard to my knife still in his midsection. Tiny put me down and said, "Come on inside and get you something to eat. I was just about to cook us something."

After eating we all sat around the house while they shared some of their favorite memories from back when Bella was younger and a few stories of when they were kids themselves. Carl even pulled out his banjo and Tiny played the harmonica. Bella and Honee danced around the house with each other. It didn't take long for Bella to reach out for me to take her hand and join the two of them. It had been many years since I had danced. After losing my entire family in that horse stable when I was sixteen, I hadn't had much reason to dance. But I didn't let that stop me from accepting her invitation to do a little boot scooting. We were all dancing and spinning around when Bella just slowed down then came to a stop, all of a sudden. Things were going great until the brothers struck up a tune that seemed to have taken Bella back to some of her childhood memories. She took a seat at the table that was placed in the middle of the room. When Bella stopped, we all stopped. I walked over to her and placed my hand on her shoulder then asked her "Are you ok"? She didn't answer me. She just put her hand on top of mine and held her head down. "That was one of daddy's favorite tunes." Honee stated with pride as she walked over to help me console Bella. The two brothers were left standing in the middle of the floor looking confused. Honee caressed Bella's back and turned to the brothers then said, "She just found out that daddy passed away." The brothers looked back at each other and nodded their heads understanding the sudden solemn mood. They walked over to join us and Carl stood on the other side of Bella then put his arm around her and said, "It's ok little one. Daddy's in a better place now. He lived a good life with no regrets." Bella looked up at Carl then smiled and looked around the room at the rest of us and gave us all one of her beautiful smiles. Tiny took a seat at the table with Bella and said with a comforting smile, "Look at the bright side. You still got us." Honee lightened the mood by adding, "You're supposed to be cheering the girl up." We all laughed and Bella seemed to be fine again.

That night during dinner Carl, Tiny and Honee shared with me a few more childhood stories about Bella. They talked about how Bella and Honee were so much alike. They told me how Honee took Bella under her wing and taught her everything that Bella knew. By the time Honee finished with Bella she could out shoot, out rope, out hunt and out ride most men. Everyone was finished with their dinner and sitting back watching big Tiny finish off his third helping. He took the last of his biscuit and wiped his plate clean with it then tossed it in his mouth. He turned to Bella and said, "That reminds me of the first time I went hunting with your daddy. Ronnie could shoot the eye out of a frog. I once saw that sum bitch drop a deer…" Tiny's story was cut short when Bella's facial expression changed and she asked him, "You want to run that by me again? What did you just say?" The house got so quiet that you could hear a fly pissing in a corner. Tiny and Carl both looked dumbfounded while Honee's eyes grew bigger than watermelons and Bella's face was as red as the inside of one. "What? All I said was how your…" Tiny started to say before being interrupted again but by Honee this time. Honee turned to Tiny and said, "I think you have your stories mixed up little brother." Then she turned back to Bella but before she could even get a word out Bella shook her head and said, "Mmmm mmmm. Tiny might be a lot of things but he's not crazy. What's going on here?" Carl looked at Honee and asked, "He never told her huh? And I'm guessing this is the first she's heard huh?" Bella jumped up out of her seat then slammed both of her hands on the table so hard that two of the plates flipped completely over. She glared at each of us holding our heads down trying to avoid direct eye contact then shouted, "Someone better get to talking or I'm heading back to the ranch right now to get some answers." No one moved a muscle or said a word. Bella slung her chair from behind her and started stomping towards the door to leave no doubt but was stopped by Honee before she could reach it. Honee rushed to the front of the door and grabbed both of Bella's hands and said, "Wait! Come have a seat and I'll explain everything to you." Although Bella was furious, Honee was able to get her to walk back to the table where the brothers and I had jumped to our feet as well. We all sat back down and Bella didn't waste any time. "Well…I'm listening!" Bella snapped. Honee snapped back "Now I know that you're pissed right now but you watch your tone of voice with me young lady. I thought you knew too until Ronnie brought me to see you." Bella's scowl slowly turned into a pout as though she had been scolded by her mother. Honee reached across the table to hold Bella's hands but Bella pulled them away then just stared at the door. Honee slowly pulled her hands back and said, "That's fine." It was obvious that it hurt Honee, but she sat there and explained everything to Bella. She even told her how Ron wanted and tried to tell her and how he made Honee promise not to tell it before he did himself. None of that mattered to Bella. She still felt betrayed by everyone including me. No one could blame her. How could we? It was a lot to handle. When Honee finished telling her everything Bella jumped up then ran into Carl's room and locked herself in. I jumped up to follow her, but Carl grabbed my hand and said, "I wouldn't do that if I were you. She's hotter than firewood right now. She just needs some time alone right now my friend." I realized he was right and sat back down.

Chapter 12
Getting Back On Track

Carl, Tiny and I sat up sharing a bottle of their best batch of whiskey while I told them my story and the purpose of our visit. Honee took over Tiny's room not long after Bella rushed away. In the morning I woke up sitting at the table with my head resting on my folded arms. I looked up and the brothers were sitting at the table with me with their heads on the table the same way I woke up. Once I started stirring around at the table it didn't take long for them to start waking up as well. Surprisingly the scent of bacon and eggs filled the house but even more surprising was that it was Bella doing the cooking. She was at the stove whistling a tune and whipping up breakfast like nothing ever happened. The three of us kind of looked around at each other all confused like. "Good morning," I said to her. She turned her head to look back at us then back to her hot skillet. "Breakfast will be ready soon. You boys need to go out back and freshen up. We have business to discuss." The three of us didn't waste any time getting to our feet. We all knew that just because she wasn't cursing didn't mean that she wasn't still pissed off. Before we could get to the door Honee came bouncing in with a big smile. "What a beautiful day it is. Good morning everyone!" she announced as she tied the belt to her robe. "Good morning darling. How'd you sleep last night?" Bella responded with a big smile. Honee walked over to Bella and wrapped her arms around her from behind and said, "Like a baby." Honee then turned back to us and said "Good morning fellas.

Hey if you're going outside, can you bring me back a pale of water so that Bella and I can freshen up as well? Thanks!" We looked at each other then shook our heads and walked out together. When we got outside Carl stopped me while Tiny kept walking to the well. "So, let me get this straight. You have your own ranch with slaves and they're all white like me?" Carl asked with a look of disbelief. I smirked and answered, "Yeah! Everyone of them is just as white as you are." He looked down then back up at me and asked, "So who's to say that you wouldn't try that with me and my brother?" I gave him a little smirk then asked, "Have you ever owned any slaves?" He frowned up and said, "Fuck no and you know that! No man deserves the right to…oooooh, I see. You only want the slave owners. That's why you're going after the twins huh?" I smiled and said, "I knew you were a smart man." Carl laughed then said, "I gotta give it to you. Going after them boys is some gutsy shit. But if we can pull this off,

you'll damn sure put a hurting on the slave trade
for miles around. My daddy loaned them boys that
money years ago before he passed away. They told
him that the money was to invest in some kind of
company up north that their uncle was looking to
expand in the area. Anyway, supposedly one of the
owners passed away and put a stop to everything.
Well that didn't stop them from using the money.
Instead of using it to go into business with their
uncle, they used it to expand their own slave
business knowing good and damn well daddy
never would have approved of such. When daddy
found out what they had done he went to them.
They basically told daddy, 'fuck you and we'll pay
you when we pay you'. Well time went by and
daddy started getting sick. Daddy never told any of
us about the loan until around his last year or so
with us. He asked us not to do anything because he
knew that he didn't have much longer and just
wanted to have peace during his last days. After
daddy passed, Tiny and I confronted the two at

their office in town. Needless to say, we haven't collected…yet. They claimed that they paid daddy but daddy wouldn't have lied to us about some shit like that for no reason. That just wasn't the kind of man he was. The conversation got a little heated in the office of course. About four or five of their men rushed in with their guns drawn and forced us to leave. That was almost six months ago now. Tiny and I figured that we would give them a little time to think that we have let it go then go back without smiling if you know what I mean. So, whatever you got planned, you can count us in!"

Bella spent the better part of the day ignoring everyone except for Honee. Neither of us was too eager to cross her anyway. We understood that she was hurt and felt betrayed. Tiny eventually came up with a great suggestion to go hunt some food for dinner. The brothers and I headed out to check a few traps they set before we came. We figured that would give Bella a little more time to calm down and get us out of harm's way. We returned a few hours before sunset with three rabbits from their traps. That would be enough to hold us over before hitting the trail back to the ranch in the morning. When we rode up to the house Bella was on the side of the house chopping up wood for the stove while Honee toted the pieces into the house. She was swinging that ax pretty strong and steady which let me know that she was no calmer than when we left. The three of us got off of our horses and Tiny decided that he would press his luck. He headed to Bella with the rabbits held high to show her what we brought back. "Hey Bella, look here at what we…," he started saying until Bella raised her ax high in the air then came down on top of the huge chunk of wood with the blade. "Aaaaugh!" she yelled out as the blade of the ax split the wood clean down the middle with that one blow. A piece of wood that size would normally require at least two chops to bust open. The chop was so violent that it made Tiny jump back and drop one of the rabbits. The blade of the ax was lodged into the ground. Bella stood there with her hands still gripping the handle. Tiny quickly grabbed up the rabbit and high tailed it back over towards the house walking fast and looking back the whole way. The look on his face drove Carl and me to knee slapping laughter until Bella turned and looked our way. That's when the laughing stopped immediately then we hurried up and got busy unpacking the trapping gear. Honee stepped out onto the porch and said, "I suggest you boys hurry on into this house before your own wood is next." We didn't waste any time taking her advice.

After dinner Bella was in no better place than she was when she first found out that Ron was her father. She helped Honee clean up the kitchen while the boys and I took a bottle outside too avoid the awkward silent treatment from Bella. Carl and I took a seat on the top step of the porch and Tiny sat in the only chair on the porch. "So how long do you think she's going to be mad at us?" I asked

Carl. He shook his head and answered "Hard to say. She can be pretty stubborn. But I'm sure I don't have to tell you. You should know that by now." I slowly nodded my head in agreement because he was right. She could be extremely strong willed and I did know all too well. When they were done Honee came outside to join us. "Where's Bella?" Carl asked Honee. Tiny stood and let Honee have his seat. She sat down and said, "Well she's gone to the room. I wouldn't be so eager to see her just yet. She and I talked and she's coming around. Give her a little more time. That was a hard pill to swallow, but she'll come around." We all kind of lowered our heads a little in disappointment. Just then we all heard the sound of a horse and cart riding up to the house. The next sounds heard were the four of us pulling out our pistols and aiming them out into the dark. Then out of the night appeared a horse pulling a cart with a well-dressed white man driving. "Thomas, what in the hell are you doing all the way out here this time of night?" Carl asked the man. The man pulled his cart to a complete stop and just sat in his seat staring at me. "Never mind that. What's THAT doing here? And why does IT have a gun...and got it pointed at me?" Thomas responded. "You don't tell me what to mind when it comes to my damn house. This is my FRIEND and he has a name and it's Cody. He's not a 'THAT' nor an 'IT'. Now I'm going to ask you one more damn time and if I don't like the next thing that comes out of your mouth, I'm going to let my FRIEND here blow your little pansy ass all the way back to your saloon. Now why are you here? We weren't expecting you for at least another week or two," Carl answered as he stood. He started walking towards Thomas with his gun still drawn. Nervously Thomas adjusted his derby hat then pushed his glasses up more with his index finger and said, "Well I'm not used to you having...friends around when I come." Carl cocked his pistol and said, "And I'm not used to you showing up at my damn house at night and unannounced. Now you have until the count of three to tell me what in the fuck you want or I swear for God…" Thomas cleared his throat and interrupted Carl with "I came late because I didn't have anyone to watch the saloon in order for me to come earlier. I just got the job to serve at the Matthews' twins birthday party this year. It's kind of a last-minute order but I was hoping you could fill for me tonight or within the next few days if you don't have enough on hand right now." Carl looked back at the porch and smiled at the three of us then asked Thomas, "So how much do you need?" "About twenty cases of your best batch should cover me," Thomas answered but couldn't help for glancing over at me still. He stared at me and I stared right back at his ass. Carl raised his gun and aimed at Thomas' head then asked, "Did you lose something on my porch?" Thomas rolled his eyes then turned his focus back to Carl. "Why do have…him at your house? I thought you were against slavery. So, I know you don't own him. What's going on here?" Carl walked up closer to Thomas with the barrel of his gun aimed for a definite kill shot. "Now does he look like a slave to you, dumb ass?" Carl questioned. Thomas never said a word but glanced back my way. Carl stretched his arm out closer towards Thomas and said, "Look over there again and it'll be your last look. Now I suggest you head on back to town and wait on your order before something happens to ya. I'll have your order delivered to you the day of the party. As a matter of fact, I'll bring it to your saloon personally." Thomas looked at Carl then signaled for his horse to get on their way. Carl patted the cart and said, "Not so fast there. Aren't you forgetting something?" Thomas stopped his cart then reached inside of his coat and pulled out his billfold and asked Carl, "Since this is a larger order than usual are you willing to give me a discount?" Carl lowered his pistol and said, "Nope!" Thomas was clearly surprised at Carl's answer. He said, "But this is a special occasion. It's the Matthews brothers' birthday party. Surely you know this could open new doors for you once everyone gets a taste and ask where it came from. You wash my back and I'll wash yours. You give me a good price and I'll help promote your product. It's a win-win for us both." Carl slowly raised his gun again and said, "I don't give a fuck. Pay me or you can go to the Braxton boys where you been getting that bullshit you sell in the saloon when you can't afford our shit. You thought I didn't know about that huh?" Thomas looked at Carl in even more shock but opened his billfold all the same. "That's right. Fuck you...pay me! Twenty cases motherfucker and I want every dime. Aaaaand, you're still going to let everyone know who has the best whiskey in town or I'll come to that saloon and put your ass to sleep. And the next time I hear about you going to the Braxtons instead of us I'm going to send Tiny to come bust up every bottle that didn't come from us." Carl demanded with his other hand, held out to receive his payment. Thomas paid Carl then rode off madder than a wet cat but knew that there was nothing he could do about it.

Once he was gone, we all put our guns away. Bella surprisingly came out onto the porch and asked, "Who was that I saw riding off?" Honee looked up at Bella and said, "That my dear was our invitation to the Matthews brothers' birthday party." Bella looked confused and responded, "Huh?" Honee smiled and said, "I'll tell you later. But was there something you needed darling?" Bella looked down at me still sitting on the steps then pointed at me and said, "Yeah. I need to talk to Cody in private for a moment." She started to head back into the house when Carl advised, "No no no. You don't have to go inside. You two young folks can sit right out here and talk. Us geezers will head on in and let you have some privacy." Bella came back out onto the porch and stepped aside to allow the others to enter the house. Tiny was first to head in but stopped to give Bella a big hug then stepped back and silently mouthed the words, "I'm sorry," to her. She pulled him back in and returned the hug. He walked on inside. Then Honee followed him but offered a smile to both of us before entering the house. Carl of course was the last to head inside. He stopped on the steps then leaned over and whispered in my ear, "I suggest you try to keep this conversation outside. There're no knives out here and less shit for her to hit you with. Good luck." "I heard that!" Bella said, as Carl was headed up the steps. He stopped in front of Bella and said "I know you did and we're all sorry Sugar. No one meant to upset you. We didn't know." Bella smiled and said, "I know and I forgive you, you old fart." Carl smiled and gave Bella a kiss on the forehead then walked inside of the house and closed the door behind him.

I stood up and walked onto the porch with Bella. When I walked up to her to give her a hug, she turned her head and put her hands in my chest to stop me. I was so confused and lost. She stepped back and told me, "Have a seat Cody! We need to talk!" I hadn't been in any other relationship other than with Sleeping Flower, so I hadn't had a lot of experience but I knew that didn't sound good. I took the seat as she suggested and locked my fingers together then leaned over to rest my elbows on my knees. I lowered my head and began looking at the floor of the porch to prepare myself for the scolding that I had coming to me. But before my head could drop to its lowest point Bella caught my chin with the tips of her fingers then slowly raised my head until we were looking eye to eye. She said, "Listen I'm not mad but I am disappointed Cody. If we're going to make this work and I do want it to work, we can't afford to keep secrets from one another. I don't care what it is or who is involved. In order for us…me and you, to make it, we HAVE to be able to TRUST each other Cody no matter what. I love you and I would lay down my life for you in a heartbeat. I'd follow you from here to hell if you asked. I'd even fight the devil himself…and win…for you. But only if I know without a shadow of a doubt that I can trust you. And I will do the same for you. Otherwise, I won't go another step with you." I started to get out of my seat to approach her and she put her hand out to stop me. She waited for me to sit back down then turned and took a couple of steps away from me. She stood there with her head down for a second then held it back up and said, "Since I'm demanding that you not withhold anything from me, I feel that it's only right that I should do the same. I have something that I probably should have told you long ago." She turned around to face me and said, "We have more in common than you know. I too lost a child once. I was young at the time. I never told anyone. Not even Ron knows. About a year or so after I left Honee and the boys, Ron set me up in the house and left me there. I know that he was off getting his own life in order, but I was alone and needed someone. I found that someone, but the wrong one. His name was Champy. He was a mixed breed, like myself. They called him Champy on the count of he was a fighter and undefeated until he nearly beat a white man to death with his bare hands one night. He was run out North Carolina for it. I met him in the same bar that I met you. He was as smooth of a talker as he was as good of a fighter. He wasn't afraid of anything or anyone. He loved a good fight and when he couldn't find one, he'd come looking for one from me. Well to be fair, he wasn't always bad. He started out being real nice and sweet. Then out of nowhere he started drinking and staying in the bar so much that the owner threatened to kill him if he came back on the count of how violent he got when he was drunk. Then when he couldn't get his whiskey, he started beating on me more and more. I ended up pregnant and carried her almost until she was ready to be born. Champy left out one night and came back sloppy drunk. I don't know where he got the liquor, but he was smelling like he had been swimming in the bottle. He wanted to...," Bella stopped talking and for the first time appeared to be about to cry. I started to stand, to give her a hug but she stretched her arm out shook her head and again waved me off. I sat back down while she turned around to gather herself and regain her composure.

She slowly turned back around and said, "He was way too big and strong. I fought with all I had. He started out slapping me but, when I ran he caught me. The slaps turned into punches. I fought back until he punched me in the stomach. Blood began to run down my leg like a river but that didn't stop him from hitting me. And it didn't stop him from raping me either. When I woke up my dress and bed were soaked in my own blood. The pain was unbearable. I started feeling so angry that soon I couldn't even feel anything. I looked over next to me and Champy was passed out sleeping with a smile on his face. I staggered into the kitchen leaking what little bit of fluids I had left and bleeding at the same time. When I came back to the bed, I went from one ear to the other with my hunting knife across his throat. He wasn't smiling then. He tried to sit up and I raised the point of the blade above my head with both hands and came down right into his chest with it. He fell back onto the bed and I kept stabbing from his nuts all the way up until the knife got stuck too deep into his cheek bone. That's when the contractions kicked in really strong. I rolled him out of the bed and eventually gave birth to a beautiful lifeless baby girl alone. I named her Angel. When I was able, I buried her in a field near the house and dragged Champy's body far away from my house and set fire to him. I didn't want his spirit or even his ashes anywhere near me. By the time Ron came back, my body was healed and he never was the wiser and I never told him. But I guess now that I know he's my father, I suppose I should probably tell him about the granddaughter he never knew about." Without warning, Bella took off running off of the porch and around to the back of the house. I took off behind her. When I got around to the back of the house, I found Bella on her knees crying like a child. I stopped in my tracks frozen stiff. I wasn't sure if I should approach her or leave her be. I took a chance and got down on my knees in front of her. I put my arms around her and pulled her in close to me. Her tears drenched my shirt and chest. Her deep sobbing made her body bounce. Years of pinned up pain, anger and hate all poured out from her wounded soul. I didn't say a word but simply held her instead. That kind of hurt doesn't go away over night or with one good cry but for the moment it helped ease her pain a little.

Chapter 13
The Bitter But Sweet Homecoming

The next morning we all got up just before sunrise to pack up for the ride back to the ranch. I was surprised to find out that not only did the brothers have enough bottles to fill Thomas' order but enough for ten times the amount he asked to be delivered. Although the ride back seemed to go a lot faster than the ride to the brothers' house it gave Bella and I more time alone to talk. She promised me not to kill Ron and to forgive him for not revealing his true identity as her father. Bella accepted the fact that Ron's decision not to tell her may have been bad but his intentions were good. It really took a load off of me knowing that the situation wouldn't escalate. When we arrived to the ranch, Ron and Moses were sitting on the porch playing a game of checkers while the whitestock worked the fields. When they spotted us coming up Moses jumped up and yelled into the house at Travis, "Hey boy come help me get Mr. and Mrs. Black unloaded with these guests." Ron came waddling down the steps to greet us in his usual slow motion. Moses stayed on the porch waiting for Travis to come out to help. Tiny was the first off of his horse to greet Ron. He ran over and picked Ron up off of his feet as if Ron was just a child. "Hey there old man. Long time no see," Tiny hollered out. "It's going to be even longer if you don't put me down before you squeeze me to death," Ron grunted out gasping for air. Tiny placed Ron back down then stepped back to take a good look at Ron then jokingly said, "You always were soft." Carl walked up to Ron and shook his hand then said, "It's good to see you my friend. It's been far too long." Ron nodded his head in agreement then patted Carl on the shoulder then headed for Bella and I. We were still standing at the back of the wagon unloading cases of whiskey when Ron walked up to Bella with his arms stretched out to receive a hug. "How was your trip darling," Ron asked with a big smile on his face. That quickly changed when Bella unloaded an unexpected open-handed slap that was heard all the way out into the field. It was so loud that the whitestock all froze and turned around. Even Moses and Travis were stopped in their tracks headed as they off of the porch. Ron staggered backwards and nearly fell on his ass. There's no doubt that he would have if Carl hadn't caught him just before going all the way down. I yelled, "What are you DOING?" Bella whipped around staring at me with a look of rage. "You PROMISED!" I said. She turned back to Ron and said out loud, "I promised not to kill him. Is he DEAD?" No one dared answer the obvious question to risk anymore of her wrath surfacing. Then she walked off towards the house. Moses and Travis rushed to get out of her way to allow her as much space up the steps as she wanted. "What in the hell was that for," Ron asked holding the side of his bright red face. Honee walked over and said, "She found out who her real daddy is and I'd say you got off lucky mister."

Bella was pretty quiet most of the day and the rest of us stayed as far away as possible, except for Ron. He tried several times to talk to her, but she just ignored him at every attempt. After lunch we were all sitting at the table and Ron said, "Hey Cody, I have something that I want you and Bella to see." Bella glanced over at Ron then stood up. She looked back at him then grabbed her empty plate and walked off into the kitchen. It was clear that he was hurt by her ignoring him that way. Honee got up and patted him on the back then caressed his shoulder. She looked down at the deflated old man and softly said, "She'll come around. I'll talk to her." Ron placed his hand on top of Honee's then gave it a little pat. He never turned around to look back at her but gave her a couple of quick nods with as much of a smile that he could muster up without breaking down. Honee leaned over and gave him a kiss on top of his head.

144

She grabbed the rest of the dishes then head off to join Bella in the kitchen. "So, what is it that you want us to see," I asked Ron to snap him out of it. "Huh? Oh yeah, it's outside out back," he answered, then slowly stood up and headed out. Slowly he walked towards the door in a daze. The brothers and I looked at each other and shook our heads then headed out behind him. We caught up with Ron just as he was about to round the corner of the house. When we got to the back of the house Ron stopped and stood with both hands on his sides. "You brought us out back to show me the horse stable," jokingly I asked. Ron looked up at me with a smirk then let out a loud whistle and started walking towards the stable. Again, the brothers and I looked around at each other then followed behind Ron. We hadn't taken much more than four or five steps before I was stopped by what I thought were my eyes playing tricks on me. I rubbed my eyes and blinked several times just to make sure that I wasn't imagining things. "How in the hell," I asked Ron. He turned to me and said with a smile, "The other morning after you guys left, I grabbed Charles and Jordan then we hit the woods looking for them. She wasn't easy to get." I walked up to Charles and the beautiful animal. It was the female horse that was always with my dream horse. I reached out to stroke her nose, but she backed away. I pulled my hand back and looked at Ron. "She's still a little nervous but she will make a great horse for Bella in due time. Her lover comes out to the edge of the woods every now and then looking for her. She's going to be the key to catching him for you. I call her 'Lady'. I really hope Bella likes her," he said, then lowered his head. I placed my hand on his shoulder and advised, "This just may be exactly what you need to get back in good my friend."

We made our way back around to the front of the house where Bella and Honee were both sitting in the two rocking chairs. Tiny was the first one of us up the steps of the porch then Carl. They walked on inside without saying a word to either of the ladies. Ron slowly crept up the steps and stopped in front of Bella while I stayed at the bottom of the steps leaning against the railing. He took his hat off and held it close to his chest with both hands then said, "Ummm Bella, I know that you're angry with me darling and I can't say that I blame you, but I didn't know how to tell you. You had been through so much and..." Before Ron could finish explaining Bella stood to her feet and said, "How could you? I trusted you. I've killed for you. What makes you think that you couldn't tell me who you really were...who I really am? You had no right!" Ron hung his head in shame and mumbled, "I'm sorry." Then she stormed into the house and upstairs to our room. Honee stood to follow Bella but I stopped her. "No not this time Honee. I'll talk to her this time," I told her. She nodded then placed her arms around Ron and guided him into the empty rocking chair. I rushed inside and up the stairs to the bedroom to confront

Bella. When I walked into the room Bella was sitting on the edge of the bed. I closed the door behind me and she shouted, "I don't want to talk about it!" I quickly responded, "GOOD! Because I didn't come up here to hear what you have to say. I came up here for you to listen and listen good!" She quickly whipped around to face me. She was in shock at my words and tone I'm sure. I walked over and stood in front of her then said, "That man out there loves you more than he loves his own self. He's been there for you at every turn that he could possibly be. The man that you thought for so many years was your father is the one that you should be upset with. He is the reason Ron was unable to tell you when you were a child. Had he not sold you off there's no telling how things may had turned out for you...for Ron for that matter. He was young, even younger than we are now. Not to mention the fact that he was married to a woman that wanted to have children but ultimately died before she was able. He tried his best to tell you but felt that by the time he found you that it would only bring about more pain than anything. Honee made him promise to tell you soon but her brother's big mouth ruined it. He really wanted you to know but not like this." Bella lowered her head then started twiddling her thumbs. I placed my hand under her chin and raised her head to look her in her eyes. From the look on her face I knew that she understood.

I went back outside with Ron and Honee and left Bella in the room alone with her thoughts. It wasn't too much longer before the front door opened and out stepped Bella onto the porch. She stood in front of the door and glanced down at me sitting on the top step of the porch. I nodded my head in the direction of Ron and Honee who never even looked in her direction. Bella looked down then held her head up and cleared her throat. Ron then stood to his feet and said, "Well I guess that's MY queue to clear out." He started to walk into the house but Bella placed her hand on his chest and said, "No wait. Don't leave. I have something that I want to say. No, I NEED to say. As a matter of fact, Cody and Honee I want you to stay as well." Ron took his seat and Honee and I sat up straight then turned towards Bella to give her our undivided attention. Before she could get started Carl and Tiny stepped to the front door. "This looks like we interrupted something important. We'll let you have some privacy," Carl said. Bella turned to them and said, "No, you can stay for this as well." They stepped out onto the porch to join the rest of us for Bella's announcement. Bella waited for everyone to get settled then turned her back to us. She paused for a moment then said, "First I want to apologize to you all for the way I've been behaving, especially to you Ron. And not just because I was the last to know but because I've known for years. I overheard master telling the misses the day he sold me. I was so hurt that for years I just blocked it out of my mind." There wasn't a closed mouth among us once she said that. Every one of us was standing with our jaws dropped open. Ron was so stunned that he stood up and sat back down then stood again. He looked at Bella and asked, "Why? Why didn't you say something? Things could have been so much easier and better." Bella stepped back from him and turned around as though she was ashamed. Ron walked up to her and placed his hand on her shoulder. Bella whipped around and barked, "Because I was HURT! You LEFT me and my mother there with those monsters and went on to live your life while momma and I were suffering. He KILLED MY MOTHER!" Ron broke down into tears and covered his face with both hands. "I'm sorry! I'm so sorry Bella!" Ron stated over and over. Bella slowly approached him and gave him a hug then softly said, "Don't you get it? I've always known. I just wanted you to say it. I wanted to hear you say that you are my father. I wanted to be loved as your daughter, not some hired hand or poor soul. I wanted the love of a father. That's all!" Her words turned both Ron and Honee into a well of tears. Bella fought back the tears for as long as she could but was no match. She too broke down.

Chapter 14
Training Days

Things around the ranch were kind of awkward for the next few days but eventually things gradually got back to normal. Carl and Tiny helped Ron and I with training all of the men on how to properly use a firearm. Bella and Honee started teaching the women and children how to read and write. Things were going perfectly as planned. One early afternoon Charles was working with Bella on training Lady for Bella to ride while the rest of us were finishing up our morning shooting lessons. Me, Moses, Jordan, Carl, Tiny and Ron were all walking around to the corral to see how things were going when I noticed that Lady began to buck and rebel. I looked out into the field and spotted her distraction. It was the black stallion. We all looked at each other and knew exactly what the other was thinking. Now was the perfect time to go after him. We all rushed to the stable for our horses. It was though he was waiting on the challenge. He stepped out from behind the trees and out into the open terrain. We raced out towards him and he never moved a muscle. The rest of the herd all stepped out from the trees as well. He turned to face them and rose up on his hind legs. He began neighing and kicking his front legs in the air as if to tell them, "Stay back." As commanded by their leader, about twenty wild horses all came to a halt. It was like nothing I had ever seen before. From the looks on the faces of the others, I wasn't alone. We continued to race out to him at top speed and still he did not budge. He held his ground until we were only feet away from him. That's when the chase began. He took off running at top speed towards us and in a split second made a sharp left turn right in front of us.

The daring move freaked the hell out of our horses and made them all damn near break their ankles trying to stop before he ran into one of them. He shot out even farther into the open land with speed none of our horses could match. It was amazing how fast he was and the quick turns he was able to make. If we were going to catch him, we were going to have to split up and cut him off by trying to circle him. It was a method I'd learned from the Shawnee. I directed Moses and Jordan to get on the sides of him. I sent Carl and Tiny to circle around to cut him off when Moses and Jordan forced him towards them. Since my horse was the fastest of ours, I had Ron to stay behind him while I tried to keep up with him in a neck and neck race to the brothers. Once everyone was in position, we began to close in on him with lassos in hands. Carl was the first to get his lasso around his neck then Tiny. That slowed him down enough for me to make my move. The others closed in on him and that's when I was finally able to get side by side with him stride for stride. I leaned over and grabbed one of the ropes around his neck and pulled myself onto his back. It wasn't easy with both horses galloping at top speed and the rope sliding. I knew that I had to make it because one stomp from either one of those animals could have cracked my skull like an egg if I had fallen. He nearly threw me to the ground several times, but I used every muscle in my body to hold on for dear life. He bucked and jumped until he wore himself out, but I was still on him. He eventually gave in either from exhaustion or the fact that he knew I wasn't getting off. Either way, I had him right where I wanted him. We were able to get him back to the ranch without any of us or him being hurt. When he got to the stable it was a grand reunion between him and Lady. They rubbed noses and necks like horses do to show love to one another. He even calmed down and walked into the stall without any problem.

We had a couple of days before the twins' party and all of the men were shooting ten times better than when we first started training. I even managed to get some time in on training the horses. I named mine Shadow because he was always appearing from them day or night. The only thing left was to pay Thomas a visit to discuss the delivery of his liquor and his role in our plan. We were going to need him to help out whether he wanted to or not. The night before the party Moses and I went into town with Carl and Tiny to pay Thomas a visit at his saloon. It was my first time in town and it was much bigger than I ever could have imagined. They called it Baltimore. I had not seen so many people in one place since I left New York as a child. We tied our horses down behind the saloon and entered through a back door that Carl and Tiny were accustomed to going through. Carl knocked twice on the door then three more times. A voice on the other side said, "Business or personal?" Carl responded, "Business is personal."

And then we heard the sound of the door unlock. A white man standing almost as big as Moses and Tiny opened the door for us. He gave Carl and Tiny a big hug and handshake each then looked Moses and me up and down then asked Carl, "So who's your friends?" Carl placed his hand on the guy's shoulder then turned to us and said, "This here is my good friend Cody and Moses. We're here to talk to your pansy ass boss. Is he in?" The guy chuckled and answered, "Yeah but you know he's not going to take too kindly to you bringing them with you in this way." Carl looked down then back up to the guy and said, "You know what Freddie? I really don't give a fuck." Freddie looked at me then back to Carl and said "That makes two of us. Go on back fellas." He shook Moses' hand then mine and through the door we went. The door led us down a barely lit hallway filled with the scent of tobacco smoke, whiskey and piss. The muffled sounds of loud music and even louder customers vibrated through the hallway's walls. The closer we got to the end of the hallway the more muffled the noise became.

We reached the end of the hallway passing three or four doors that must've led to different areas inside of the saloon. At the end was another door. Carl gave the door the same coded knock and a voice yelled out come in. It's unlocked." Carl opened the door then walked in and we followed him inside. When we walked in, I wasn't surprised to find Thomas sitting behind a big fancy wooden desk. I wasn't surprised at how big and nice his hideaway office was. What did surprise me was the little black girl that jumped up off of her knees from behind his desk. She stood next to him with a look of shame then used the sleeve of her dress to wipe off her mouth and face. She didn't look to be much older than Moses' daughter Asha. Thomas stood to button up his britches and fasten his belt then said with a smug, "You must've brought them with you to help unload my order. The problem is one, I don't need it until tomorrow around noon and two, you know better than to bring niggers to my office. That's a no-no." Carl looked at Tiny and they both kind of laughed. Carl said to Tiny "You hear this shit? He must've forgotten who the fuck he's talking to." Moses and I didn't laugh or even so much as crack a smile. I could see and feel the hurt in Moses' eyes. I knew that he was thinking that could have easily been what was happening to his baby girl Asha when she was alone back on their old plantation. I'm sure it brought back the memories of having to leave her just to do his old slave duties. "What's your name little lady?" Moses asked the girl. Before she could speak Thomas quickly snapped, "That's none of your fucking business!" I responded just as snappy "He wasn't talking to you!" Thomas started to walk from behind his desk until the sound of Tiny's six shooter being cocked and aimed at him brought him to a stop. "WHAT DO YOU WANT," Thomas angrily shouted. "First off we want to know this girl's name for starters." Carl answered.

Thomas smacked his desk then pointed at Carl and said, "And like I told him…" Unfortunately for him, Tiny pulled his trigger and fired his gun before Thomas could finish. Thomas' hand flew backwards and he yelled out in agony. "CONNIE MAE! My name is Connie Mae…sir," the girl answered when Tiny cocked his pistol again. Thomas held his hand while blood poured all over his desk. "That's a pretty name," Moses told her. She was so scared that I could see her little body starting to tremble in fear. "Do you have any family," Moses asked her. "No sir. Master Thomas is alls the family I has sir," she responded trembling even more. Moses waved his hand for her to come over to him. "You don't have to stay here and you definitely don't have to do what you were just doing. We have somewhere that you can live as a free person and be treated with some respect. All you have to do is come with us. I'll protect you just like I do my own daughter," Moses suggested. Connie was a little hesitant at first but took a deep breath and looked over at Thomas holding his bleeding hand then she gathered up enough courage to start walking towards Moses' opened arms. Before she could take a step, Thomas reached out and grabbed Connie Mae by the hand to stop her. That's when Moses drew his gun and fired it at Thomas. The bullet blew the hat clean off of Thomas' head and dropped to the floor. "OK OK…you can have her. Take her!" Connie Mae rushed over to Moses and threw her arms around his waist then buried her face in his chest. "Ok…you have her. She's yours but I know that's not the only reason you came out. Now what the hell do you want?" Carl took his time and slowly walked across the room then stopped in front of the desk across from Thomas. Without warning or saying a word, he reached across the desk and grabbed the hand that Thomas was shot. He squeezed and twisted Thomas' hand. Thomas yelled out in more agony. "Tomorrow morning we're coming back here with your cases of whiskey. We're going to make the delivery with you and you only. So, let whoever you normally take with you know that their services will not be needed tomorrow. We will have enough manpower to take care of this order. And if you say a word to anyone about this, it's going to be your brains blown on the floor instead of your hat." Carl demanded then tightened his grip on Thomas' hand even more. "You got that," Carl questioned. Thomas was in too much pain to speak. He nodded his head "yes" instead. Carl slammed Thomas' wounded hand on the desk and smiled at the painful look on Thomas' face. Then we left, along with Connie Mae.

Chapter 15
When The Morning Comes

That night when we got back to the ranch, I sent Bella and several of our men to set up camp right outside of town for the night. That way they would already be in position with well rested horses before we got there. The party was being held in a huge inn with a large ballroom located on the edge of town. It was a well-known spot for many local and major events in town. In the morning I rode back into town with just Carl and Tiny. Ron and Honee stayed behind with Moses and a few others to keep an eye on the whitestock while we were gone. I needed a strong presence there to keep the fear of running in the whitestock. The brothers and I reached Thomas' saloon with two covered wagons of whiskey. Tiny drove one of the wagons and I rode along with Carl in the other wagon. We arrived at the saloon long before Thomas and sat behind the saloon waiting on him to arrive as well. When he did finally arrive, he was riding on an uncovered wagon of his own with another white man commanding the reins. They stopped just a few feet in front of our wagons. "I thought I told you to come alone?" Carl sneered. "I know what you said but ole Joe here is here for my protection," Thomas responded. "Protection?

Protection from what," Carl asked. Thomas glanced over at is friend Joe. Joe looked at Carl and patted the rifle he had lying across his lap. Thomas then looked back at Carl and said, "Protection from YOU! You crazy son of a bitch." Out of nowhere the sound of a gunshot rang out and just like that...Joe was dead from a bullet through his heart. Thomas jumped backwards in his seat in shock. His face was covered with the blood and brains of his buddy Joe. "We don't have time for this shit. Now get your ass over here and get on this wagon with me or you're next!" Tiny demanded of Thomas with the barrel of his pistol still smoking. Thomas was so shaken up that he could hardly pull himself together. He was wiping his face and staring at Joe's slumped over body. Thomas was trembling so hard that he stumbled to the ground when he got off of his wagon. "Looks like you should have brought protection for your friend too," Carl said laughing at Thomas scurrying around trying to get to his feet and looking back at his dead partner. Thomas eventually took his seat next to Tiny and was still trembling like a leaf. "Now don't try anything stupid and make me kill you too," Tiny strongly urged Thomas. "Now did you tell anyone else about us going with you," Tiny asked with his pistol pressed firmly in Thomas' rib cage. "No. Just Joe. I swear!" Thomas pleaded with the fear of God in him. Tiny said, "You better not be lying!" And, then put away his gun so that we could get moving to meet the others.

Not long after leaving the saloon we were soon rejoined with Bella and the others that were waiting on our arrival. When we rode up everyone was gathered under a large shade tree loading up their sleeping gear. Bella was the first to notice us and the first to run up to greet us. I hopped off of the wagon and gave her a big hug and kiss. "I see you brought along a little company," she pointed out in regards to Thomas. "Yeah this is the saloon owner Thomas that we told you about," I explained. "Well we're all packed up here and ready to go. But what's all that on that fella's face?" she said. Carl quickly responded, "Oh that's Thomas' friend Joe. You see Thomas invited him to join us even though I asked him not to bring anyone along with him. Tiny compromised with the fella and found a way for some of old Joe to make the ride anyway. He was supposed to be Thomas' protection." Bella smirked and said, "Well from the looks of things it sounds like Joe needed some protection himself." Carl burst into laughter and said, "THAT'S what I said too!" Bella motioned to Thomas and ordered, "Well Joe's ride ends here but you have more to do. So come on down here and let me get you a wet rag to wash your protection off your face." Jordan walked up grinning like the cat that swallowed the canary and asked, "Are we really going to get to kill white folks?" He then glanced up at Carl with a bit of remorse and said, "No offense. You's good white folks. I just want to kill the bad ones. You know." Carl smiled and replied, "None taken son. None at all. Hell, Tiny just killed one today already. Hopefully we can get out of here without killing anyone. But if there's any killing needed to be done, don't you hesitate none. You hear? Just make sure it's necessary." Jordan was pleased and couldn't help for smiling even harder. Once everyone was done packing up, we headed off on our mission. It didn't take very long to get to our destination. The brothers and I took our wagons up to the back of the hotel while the others stayed hidden in the thick cover of trees that were only a few yards behind the back entrance.

Tiny and Thomas walked up to the back door while Carl and I stayed put on our wagon waiting to see what was going to happen after Thomas banged on the door a couple of times. Carl had Thomas to carry a couple of crates of the whiskey to hide the small droplets of blood on his shirt. There wasn't much but enough to notice. It wasn't long before a silver haired old black man wearing a white jacket and black pants opened the huge double doors. Thomas asked to speak to someone and the old man hurried off to fetch the person as told. A clean-cut white man dressed in a grey suit walked out onto the back deck to greet Thomas. They spoke for a bit then Carl shook hands with the man and the three of them headed inside. Carl waved out to us to let us know that it was ok to start unloading the rest of the whiskey as well as to set our plan in motion. While we were unloading the crates, the others took their positions and waited for the signal from me. Carl managed to strike up conversation about hunting and fishing with the guy. It created the perfect distraction. Carl kept complimenting on how nice the place was, so the guy offered to give us a quick tour of the hotel after we finished unloading. Just as we were making our last round the guy was called away for something by one of the workers. He excused himself and suggested that we could take a look around for ourselves when we were done. He said he would find us when he was done. The moment he was out of sight I rushed away to take my chance to peek into the main lobby. I took Carl with me just in case we spotted the twins, considering I didn't know the men. I have to admit, the place was so beautiful that I was mesmerized for a moment. I was snapped out of my spell when Tiny said, "That's them right there." I whipped my head around in the direction he was looking. I was surprised to see that they looked nothing like what I was expecting. There stood two of the dumpiest white men I had ever seen. They were about Bella's height and rounder than a child's ball. "That's them? Those two little sawed off shits?" I asked holding back my laughter. He looked over his shoulder with a smile and nodded. "Do you like what you see?" a voice said from behind us. We both slowly turned to see that the guy came back as he said he would. "Yes sir. I'm loving what I'm seeing," I responded. He turned his nose up at me and said, "Well I'm quite sure you are boy. You could probably put a hundred slave shacks like yours in a place this size." I could feel my own eyes lower. Before I could say or do anything Carl snapped at him. "His name is Cody!" The guy jumped in shock at the obvious attitude change in Carl. It was then he realized something wasn't right. "Well forgive me. I didn't know you were so protective of your help. Around here we find that it's best not to get too attached to our niggers." He jumped again and bucked his eyes when I shoved the barrel of my pistol in his side. He looked back around to me with his mouth wide open. "I'm no one's nigger! I'm DAMN sure not anyone's slave. But you, you are about to be our help," I growled at him. Carl and I walked the guy back through the kitchen area to get to the backdoor. The three of us walked outside with my gun firmly shoved in the guy's back. Everyone was so busy working that no one even noticed us walking out. When we got outside Tiny was waiting on us with Thomas already tied up in the back of his covered wagon. "Everyone is already in position and waiting" Tiny advised. "That's good. Now all we have to do is get Mr. Kitchen Man here to get the twins away from everyone else and we're home free before anyone recognizes that they're gone," Carl said standing so close to the man that the brim of his hat was poking the guy in the forehead.

Chapter 16
Go Time

Once I confirmed that everyone was in place Carl, Tiny and I walked the guy back inside. The workers were still just as busy as before. "Are you important enough around here to have an office," I asked the nervous fellow. "Y…y…yes. It's on the o…o…other side of the k…k…kitchen near the entrance to the main lobby" he responded with a bit of stuttering. Carl faced the man and smiled. He placed his hand on the guy's shoulder and calmly said, "Heeeey, relax. This will all be over before you know it." The guy dropped his head and began to tune up like he was about to start crying. "Look you don't have anything to worry about as long as you don't call my friend here another nigger and you do exactly what we say. You'll be just fine." The guy slowly raised his eyes to Carl and did his best to get himself together. "That's it. Just breathe and relaaaax," Carl continued. "Now all you have to do is get one of your workers to have Harry and Terry Matthews come to your office and we'll handle the rest from there. By the way, I never got your name. I'm Carl, this here is my brother Tiny and of course you've met Cody already," Carl said in a soothing tone. The fellow regained his composure then stuck chin and chest out and said, "My name is Wyatt." Carl patted him on the chest and said, "Now see, we're all friends now. Now Wyatt, I need you to find someone to fetch those twins and have them brought to your office to discuss a problem with tonight's menu. Do you think you can do that without raising any suspicion?" Wyatt gave a couple of quick nods, but it was obvious that he was still scared shitless. He cleared his throat then turned in the direction of the workers and waved his hand to someone nearby to come to him. A young black man came trotting over with no delay. "Jasper, do you know who this party is for," Wyatt asked the young man. "Oh yesuh," the young man responded. "Splendid. I need you to find them and escort them both to my office to discuss an issue with tonight's menu. It's very urgent. So, hurry along and find them," Wyatt ordered. Again, the young man wasted no time doing as told. "I knew you could do it," said Carl as he placed his arm around Wyatt's shoulder. "I bet you have a bottle of some kind of expensive hooch in that office of yours. Let's go have a drink. You look like you could use a good drink right about now" Carl suggested as we headed to Wyatt's office.

We patiently waited in Wyatt's office for the twins to arrive. Wyatt took a seat behind his desk while Carl and Tiny sat in two chairs across from him with their backs to the door. I on the other hand chose to stand by the door. We heard a knock on the door. Before Wyatt could respond the door flew open and in marched the twins madder than two rattlesnakes on fire. They rushed in yelling and swearing at Wyatt to the top of their voices so fast that they never noticed me. Carl and Tiny both stood up and turned around to face the twins. That immediately put a stop to all of their hollering. "What in tarnation is going on here," asked one of the twins. "Why in the hell are you two here," asked the other. Then they heard the clicking sound from me cocking my two pistols. "Ok, what in the HELL is going on here Carl? What are you and Tiny doing here? Who the FUCK is this nigger? Why does he have goddamn guns pointed at us," yelled one of the twins pointing his finger back and forth from Carl to me. Carl burst into laughter then clapped his hands together and said, "The look on you two fuckers' faces is priceless.

Hell, it's worth even more than the money you owe my family." The other twin turned to Wyatt and asked, "Do you mind tell us what the fuck is going on here?" Wyatt shrugged his shoulders and shook his head but had no words to offer. "You see Terry, that's your problem. You're asking the right questions but the wrong person," Carl said while still laughing. They both turned to face me as they should have from the beginning considering I was the one with the guns on them. "My name is Cody...Cody Black. I understand you two men are supposed to be the biggest slave traders in the area?" I said with my guns still aimed at both of their chest. "And? What's it to you? And what do Carl and Tiny have to do with any of that?" Harry yelled back, "First of all, you need to take some of that bass out of your voice when you speak to me!" I advised, stretching my arm out to aim for his head. "Who do you think you are?" Terry responded with a snarl. I stretched my other gun out and aimed for his head also then said, "I'm your new master. Now say ONE more word and I'll be the man that sent you to meet your Maker." They both damn near swallowed their own tongues. "And we're here to collect our money and make sure that our friend Cody here gets back home safely," Carl added. They were obviously unaware of what I had in store for them and that's exactly what I wanted. They had all of the explanation they needed at the moment.

Tiny went back outside to signal the others that we were ready to come out and to set the next step of the plan in motion. Carl tied up the twins' and Wyatt's hands while we waited for a sign for us to exit the building. "Whatever he's paying you, I know damn well we can afford to pay you twice as much. It can't be that much. Fuck it, we'll triple it. Hell, he's a nigger for God's sake. He can't have much money if any," Terry pleaded with Carl. His pleading found the back of my hand to his face landing him on the floor with his hands behind his back, unable to break his fall. I calmly stood over him and pointed my pistol at his face and said with a smile, "Call me another nigger! I dare you!" Needless to say, he shut the hell up. Carl pulled him to his feet then gagged all three of them with pockets torn from their own jackets and tied with their belts so that they could no longer speak. Then, all of a sudden we all heard a loud explosion ring out outside, "BOOM." Wyatt and the twins jumped with fear and began to panic. "BOOM!" rang out another explosive bang. The commotion from panicking workers on the other side of the office door went from a loud chatter to all out chaos. "BOOM…BOOM…BOOM," went more explosions. That was our signal to haul ass out of the office to where the others were waiting. We darted out into the rushing crowd of workers and blended in without anyone noticing the three men tied and gagged. Everyone was out for themselves. People were everywhere running for their lives. We dragged the three of them through the kitchen and just as we got to the backdoor, I spotted someone from my past that nearly brought me to a complete stop. "KEEP GOING! KEEP GOING!" coming from Carl shouting at me from behind kicked me back in motion. We ran through the backdoor and rushed down to the wagon Tiny had waiting for us. "BOOM! BOOM! BOOM…," went more explosions. Carl and I rushed the three men into the back of the empty wagon. I hopped into the back with them and covered the back. Carl got up front with Tiny. We took off like a bat out of hell. The other wagon with Thomas inside had already been taken away by the others. I peeked out from the back cover to see if anyone was following us or if I could spot any of our people. There were people everywhere running and screaming outside of the huge burning building. I saw the other three wagons across the field racing away and heading back into the woods just like us. The only difference was that they were being shot at by a few white men that were running behind the wagons. Bella and the guys ran off all of the horses that were outside then lit sticks of dynamite in the stagecoaches and wagons that weren't ours. Luckily my four best shooters that were placed in the edge of the woods were able to pick off most of the men one by one and forced the rest to turn back. They made sure that the wagons made it back to the woods before retreating. It was an amazing sight to see but it was nothing compared to the man I saw before running out of the backdoor. I couldn't believe my eyes. Although it had been years since I had seen him, he hadn't changed much. From the look on his face when we locked eyes, I know he recognized me as well. I hadn't changed that much more either. But why was he there, was the biggest question of all.

Chapter 17
I Can't Believe It

We all split up once we got into the woods just in case anyone was chasing us. Everyone made it all the way back to the ranch without anyone following us. Moses, Ron and Honee came out to welcome us back home as we all arrived moments after each other. Bella's wagon was the last of the group to ride up. I was in the middle of unloading the twins and Wyatt when Bella's wagon came up with her steering the rumbling wagon. "I NEED SOME HELP OVER HERE! HE'S BEEN SHOT!" Bella yelled out as she brought the wagon to a stop. That's when I discovered that all of us didn't make it back unharmed. Moses rushed over to her wagon asking, "WHO? Who was shot? Where is he?" Bella hopped down then raced to the back of the wagon with Moses on her heels. We all ran over to them to see who she was talking about. Before anyone else could get there, Moses had already reached into the back to help get whoever it was out. I wasn't quite close enough yet to see which one of the men it was, but I was rushing over as fast as my legs could carry me. By the time I got over there Moses had gently laid him on the ground and a crowd formed around them keeping me from seeing. Moses and Bella were kneeling down over the person. I forced my way through the growing crowd to get a look to see who was on the ground. My heart dropped when I saw that it was young Jordan laying there with a bullet wound to his stomach. He was coughing up blood by the cupful and gasping for air. His shirt and trousers were soaked in his own blood. He struggled to speak. "Don't try to speak. Save your breath and stay with me Jordan," Moses begged with pain in his voice. He was also struggling to fight back his tears trying to be strong for Jordan. Jordan reached up for Moses with his hand trembling. Moses took a hold of his hand with both of his and held it. It wasn't looking good. Jordan then looked up at me and said in a very weak voice "I got…one…of those bastards Cody." Then he looked back at Moses and said, "I wish… you could have… seen it." He coughed a couple of times and his eyes fluttered. Then he closed his eyes and just like that, he was gone. "NOOOOO!" Moses cried out. He wrapped his large arms around Jordan then laid his head on Jordan's chest and cried like a baby.

The next day we buried Jordan on a hill not far from the ranch. I had not known him nearly as long as Moses knew him but in the short time that I did have with him made me extremely attached. As much as his death weighed on me, I couldn't forget about who I saw in the kitchen at the inn. If it was who I thought, I needed some answers and the twins were the only ones that could possibly tell me what I needed to know. After supper that night I had the twins brought to me in the horse stables. Moses, Tiny and Carl joined me as they had matters of their own to settle with the twins. The twins were dragged into the stables cursing and resisting with every step. "Tie each of them to a pole facing it," I told the men that brought them in. They yelled and threatened all of us, but it didn't stop them from getting tied nor stop what was about to happen. "Enough!" Carl yelled out. Carl walked over to Harry and said, "I don't want to hear another fucking word from either of you unless you're telling me about our money!" Terry blurted out, "Is that what this is all about? MONEY? You let some nigger talk you into signing your death warrant over money? You won't get a DIME!" Carl walked over to him and grabbed him by the back of his head and asked, "Is that sooo?" Terry struggled to turn his head as far around as he could to look Carl in the eye and said, "You're damn right it's so!" Carl slammed his face into the pole then let him go. Carl started walking back over to us and said, "We'll see about that." Tiny grabbed a horse whip from the wall and stood behind the other twin. I walked over to the twins and pulled out my knife. Then I cut open both of their jackets and shirts down the middle to expose their bare backs. Harry's knees started to shake together so bad that they were knocking. "You can't do this! You don't whip white folks. That's for niggers!" he pleaded as I was walking away. His words stopped me in my tracks. I turned back to him and said, "You mean niggers like me?" He didn't say anything. "You're damn right! Niggers just like you," his brother yelled out. "You might be onto something there. Maybe this is something for a nigger like me," I said back. I walked up to Tiny and asked with my hand out, "Do you mind?" Tiny handed me the whip with a smile and said, "Be my guest." I took the whip and walked over to Moses. I handed the whip to Moses and said, "Actually I think you are the kind of nigger he was talking about." Moses took the whip and gripped it so hard that it was making a squeaking sound in his hand. The anger in his eyes was strong, so strong that it sent a chill down my spine. Slowly he walked up behind them mumbling, "This is for Jordan."

Moses was full of anger over Jordan's death as we all were. He used the whip to try not only to beat them but to try to literally destroy their bodies. Terry was the first to feel his wrath. He took turns giving each of them five harsh lashes across their bare backs before moving to the other. He was heading back to Harry for the third time before Harry broke down crying and begging for mercy. Mercy was not what Moses was there to offer and so none was given. His cries seemed to fuel Moses and his whip, "PLEEEEASE! PLEEEEASE FOR THE LOVE OF GOD, STOP! STOP! STOOOOP!" Harry begged. "THAT'S ENOUGH DAMN IT! LEAVE HIM ALONE! Please just leave him alone." Terry began to plead for his brother. Moses paused and looked over at Terry then drew back and began thrashing Harry even harder. The blood from Harry was splashing all over the pole he was tied to and began to pour from his back to his feet. In great pain Harry could no longer take anymore. He dropped to his knees with his tied hands wrapped around the pole and extended above his head. He slumped over and passed out. "HARRY…HARRYYYYY! YOU

MOTHERFUCKERS! YOU KILLED MY BROTHER! HARRYYYY!" Terry screamed. I walked over to Harry and gave him a good slap across the face to bring him to. "He's not dead…yet. But he will be if you don't pay these men and answer a few questions that I have. Then I'm going to let Moses take you out the same way," I told him. Terry knew that his brother couldn't stand anymore so he gave up. He told Carl and Tiny everything that they needed to get money from their safe in their office back in town. He gave them the combination to their safe and also told them just how to get in and out without getting caught. More importantly to me, he confirmed that the man I saw was who I thought he was…my father's old business partner, Jefferson Reed.

Chapter 18
The Jack of All Trades

Apparently business fell off for Jefferson not long after my father passed. He decided to go into the slave trading business. He had built a small fortune taking free blacks down south against their wills and passing them off as runaways. According to Terry, they were planning to become business partners with Jefferson. He was in town not only to celebrate their birthdays but to also sign off on a deal that was going to make them all rich. Carl and Tiny got up early the next morning to head back into town to get their money. They didn't want to waste too much time. They knew the town's sheriffs would be on high alert after everything that happened the day before. They suggested that I stay back at the ranch considering the twins being seen taken by a black man. They were right. It just wasn't safe for me but there was no way in hell I was going to pass up the opportunity to confront

Jefferson face to face. Jefferson was scheduled to meet with the twins and their attorney Benjamin Taylor to sign some last-minute contracts to seal their deal. The meeting was scheduled for noon. That was just enough time to get into town to hit the office for the money and be at the attorney's office before Jefferson. I was sure that the word had gotten around that the twins were missing. That meant Jefferson wouldn't be sticking around for long. So, I had to get to him before he left town. There was also the possibility that Jefferson would leave town without even going to the attorney's office. It was a long shot of a chance. But one thing was certain, and that was that I definitely wouldn't get to see him if I did not go. Charles had been working with Shadow to get him ready for riding. This was as good of a time as any to take him with me. He was way faster than any of the other horses we owned and there was no room for error with a slower horse. When I went to the stable to get Shadow ready for our ride, I found

Bella already inside and saddling up her horse Lady. "What are you doing," I asked. Without stopping what she was doing she quickly responded, "What does it look like I'm doing? I'm doing what you need to be doing. If my man is going to fight, then I'm going with him. Get your horse ready and let's go." She never took her eyes off of what she was doing until she heard me take a breath to speak. She whipped her head around before I could make a sound then gave me a look that could only be understood as "I wish you would fix your mouth to tell me I can't go." I closed my mouth and started getting Shadow ready because we didn't have time for me to try to talk her out of it. Plus, I knew there was no stopping her anyway.

Shadow and Lady did fine with the ride to town. We arrived at the back of the twins' office and the door was locked as expected. Fortunately, Terry was kind enough to tell us where to find the hidden spare key, not that he had much choice.

Carl and Tiny made it inside with no problem. They made it back out with two bags of money in each of their hands while Bella and I stayed outside to keep a look out for anyone coming. We were all mounted on our horses ready to ride off when we heard a voice yell out from behind us. "Hey wait!" they yelled. We turned around and there was a middle aged well-dressed white man running from around the front of the building waving his hands above his head. "Wait…wait!" he continued yelling and waving for us to stop. "Well well, what a surprise if it isn't attorney Taylor. What are you doing here," Carl questioned the man. He gave a nervous smile and said with concern, "I came to see if the twins may have shown up by chance. I have a meeting scheduled with them in less than an hour and they're always early for these types of things. The word around town is that they went missing. Some even say they were abducted by some black fellow. I was hoping you might have seen them by chance." We all gave him a dumbfounded look and shrugged our shoulders. "We were kind of hoping to find them here too. Tiny and I have a little unfinished business with them ourselves. But if we see them, we'll be sure to let them know you're looking for them also," Carl answered. The man hung his head then looked up and said, "I'm afraid by then it may be too latte perhaps. I have their out of town business partner on his way to my office now. If I don't find them soon, he's going to be on the next train back to New York. Then there will be no deal. I have to get back to my office and try to buy more time," the attorney responded. He turned and started walking back around to the front of the office.

That bit of information was just what we needed. It confirmed that I was right about my hunch. Jefferson Reed was still in town planning to close their slave trade agreement. We needed to hurry if we were going to get to the office before Jefferson. We rode fast and hard to get there.

There was a saloon across the street from the attorney's office. We got there with plenty of time to spare. We tied our horses down behind the saloon. Before we headed inside, I stopped the brothers and said, "Listen, you don't have to stay. I got it from here. Besides, you have a lot of money tied to those horses; too much to be left unattended while I settle an old score that has nothing to do with you. You fellas go ahead and get out of town with it while you still can." They looked at each other then back at me and Bella. Then Carl asked, "Are you sure?" I placed my hand on his shoulder and said with a smile "I'm sure." Carl reached out and gave me a big hug then stepped back and said, "If there's ever anything that you need, you know where to find us my friend." He stepped over to Bella then hugged her and said, "My little Bella. What a fine woman you grew up to be. You take good care of this man and yourself. I'm proud of the woman you've become, and I will see you two again soon." Then he got onto his horse. Tiny shook my hand then yanked me into his big arms for one of his famous bear hugs. "You take care of our Bella. She means a lot to us," he said. Then he stretched his arms out and Bella fell right into them. "You take care of YOURSELF, you big old bear. I will be to see you guys soon," Bella said with a lump in her throat. Tiny leaned over and kissed her on top of the head then said to her, "You better." Tiny rushed onto his horse to fight back his tears. We all looked at each other one more time then they turned and rode off.

Bella and I ordered a couple of shots of whiskey from the bar of the saloon then took a seat near a window so that we could keep an eye on the attorney's office. Carl was right about one thing. The tension in the air was pretty thick in the saloon. It was obviously coming from the commotion we caused the day before. It was also obvious that no one knew exactly what happened or else we would have been strung up as soon as we stepped inside. It was a risk that we were willing to take. Luckily the attorney finally rode up and went inside of his office. A few moments later a fancy stagecoach rode up as well. Then out from the stagecoach stepped Jefferson Reed himself. He walked into the office followed by another much younger man. The driver of the stagecoach got down and walked off. That was our queue to head over to the office ourselves. Bella and I got up and headed for the door but were stopped by three men that blocked our path. "Look fellas we don't want any trouble. My lady and I are about to leave," I tried to explain. I didn't have time for their bullshit. So, I tried to be nice but they weren't trying to hear it. "I don't think I've ever seen you two around here before," one of them said with a snarl. "I know damn well I've never seen them and I'm here every day!" another man snapped. "What's your name boy?" the second man continued. The third fellow never said anything, but he had that look in his eye that I'd seen in plenty of white men. He wasn't the kind of man that was much for words. I noticed his hand slowly moving towards the gun on his hip. "Like I said, I don't want any trouble. Just let us leave and we'll be on our way." I told them. "And he asked you a question" the first man said. They started to slowly walk towards us and I knew then that it was about to get ugly. Bella put her hand in her purse and quickly pulled out her two-shot derringer and pointed it at the men. That stopped them in their tracks and slowly they raised their hands. "You only have two bullets and there're three of us," the third man finally said. Before I could pull my gun to even the odds the saloon door flew open and slammed against the wall. The very next sounds were from two rifles cocking with Carl holding one and Tiny holding the other. "What seems to be the problem," Carl asked the three men. "And who the fuck are you," asked the first guy. Carl walked up to him and placed the barrel of his rifle on the man's forehead then said, "I'm the crazy sum bitch with a rifle. And from that there window it looked like you were having a problem with my friends here." Carl looked at the other two men then back at the first guy and said, "Now I'm going to ask you one more time. Do we have a problem here?" The man turned his head and spat his tobacco spit on the floor then said, "Naw! There's no problem." Carl smiled and said, "Good! So, step aside so my two friends can attend a rather important meeting while the rest of us sit here until they're done. You don't mind, do you?" The guy shook his head no then stepped aside for Bella and me. Carl and I gave each other a nod as I walked past him and patted him on the shoulder. Bella put away her pistol as she walked up to Tiny and said, "I sure am glad to see you two." He smiled and said "We figured you might need a hand. So, we stashed our things and came back to check on you." She kissed him on the cheek and we walked out leaving them inside.

Bella and I were halfway into the busy street headed to the attorney's office when the office door opened. It was Jefferson and the guy that walked inside with him. They were obviously upset about the absence of the twins. Attorney Taylor was rushing out behind them screaming, "I'm sure there's a logical explanation!" Jefferson stopped and quickly turned to the attorney then yelled, "I saw them with my own eyes you idiot! WHY would I want to do business where you allow niggers to steal not one but TWO white men from their own birthday party for God's sake? Tell me! I came here hoping that they would be here but clearly they are NOT!" He turned and started back walking towards his stagecoach where his driver was waiting for the two. We got a few feet closer but were stopped by a slow-moving horse and cart driven by a family of white folks. They were in no hurry and unbothered at the fact that they were in our way. By the time they cleared our path the young man had made it inside of the coach. Jefferson had his hand and one foot on the coach about to pull himself up to get inside.

"JEFFERSON REED!" I yelled out. He stopped then turned to face me. He stepped down and stood there staring as if he had seen a ghost. I guess in his mind I probably was a ghost to him. He probably thought that I was killed years ago with the rest of my family. "Cody? Is that you," he asked walking towards us as another horse and buggy crossed our paths. "Yes!" I answered back. "What are you doing here? That WAS you that I saw in the kitchen yesterday wasn't it," he asked as I walked closer. "It was. But I could ask you the same. What are you doing here? Or better yet, why are you in the slave trading business now?" The younger man with him stuck his head out of the window of the stagecoach and yelled out, "Father, who are they?" His words stopped all three of us in our tracks. I knew that Jefferson had a son around my age, but I had never met him. He turned to his son and said, "I'll be there in a moment." He turned back to us and said, "Look I can explain." But before he could say another word gunfire rang out from behind Bella and me. We all ducked and turned to see what was going on. Then another shot sounded off. It was coming from the saloon Carl and Tiny were in. All of a sudden, Carl and Tiny came running out from behind the saloon on in their wagon. Tiny was driving and Carl was firing behind them at some men chasing them. I looked back around and Jefferson was running to his stagecoach. Carl and Tiny were approaching us fast and had both of our horses with them. There was no time for chasing after Jefferson. Carl and Tiny needed our help. Bella and I started firing at the men chasing them and ran as fast as we could to catch up to our horses. Tiny turned a corner and slowed down just enough for Bella to get onto his wagon. Shadow was headed straight for me as if he knew to come get me. Shadow turned the corner with Tiny. I jumped to grab the saddle horn then I stuck my foot in the stirrup and with one strong kick off, I pulled myself up then swung my leg over Shadow's back. Bella's horse Lady was running neck and neck with us as we raced out of town with white men gunning for our heads. The busy streets worked to our advantage. With so many people everywhere, the men didn't shoot for long. We made it out of town alive but that meant so did Jefferson and his son. That didn't sit well with me at all. This was the man that my father suggested that I go to for help if I needed it. I had questions and I was determined to get answers. Even if that meant going back to New York to find Jefferson then that's what I was going to do.

To be continued...